"Don't be Cute!"

Nick frowned at his choice of words. She *was* cute, dammit, that was exactly the problem. The closer he'd gotten, the better Randy looked. Those million-dollar legs of hers weren't helping matters one bit! How on earth could he be expected to concentrate on what he wanted to say? He uttered a low, frustrated growl and let his eyes skim down over her once more.

"Surely," Randy said sweetly, "you didn't come all the way out here just to object to my physical attributes?"

To her surprise, Nick's eyes glittered with unexpected warmth. "Believe me, Miss Wade," he said softly, his voice humming with a throaty undercurrent that seemed to stroke her senses, "it's not your body I find objectionable, by any means!"

Dear Reader:

SILHOUETTE DESIRE is an exciting new line of contemporary romances from Silhouette Books. During the past year, many Silhouette readers have written in telling us what other types of stories they'd like to read from Silhouette, and we've kept these comments and suggestions in mind in developing SILHOUETTE DESIRE.

DESIREs feature all of the elements you like to see in a romance, plus a more sensual, provocative story. So if you want to experience all the excitement, passion and joy of falling in love, then SILHOUETTE DESIRE is for you.

For more details write to:

Jane Nicholls
Silhouette Books
PO Box 236
Thornton Road
Croydon
Surrey CR9 3RU

LAURIEN BLAIR
Taken by Storm

Silhouette Desire
Originally Published by Silhouette Books
division of
Harlequin Enterprises Ltd.

First published in Great Britain 1986 by Silhouette Books, 15–16 Brook's Mews, London W1A 1DR

© Laurien Blair 1985

Silhouette, Silhouette Desire and Colophon are Trade Marks of Harlequin Enterprises B.V.

ISBN 0 373 05243 X

22–0486

Made and printed in Great Britain for Mills & Boon Ltd by Richard Clay (The Chaucer Press) Ltd, Bungay, Suffolk

LAURIEN BLAIR

writes, "I am having a great time writing romances because they are one of the few mediums in which you can construct a perfect world, and the ending is always happy. The other thing I hope readers will find in my books is a sense of fun. My characters are going to laugh a lot, love a lot and have a great time, for in the end, that's really what I think falling in love is all about."

Other Silhouette Books by Laurien Blair

Silhouette Desire

Sweet Temptation
Between the Covers
A Touch of Magic

For further information about Silhouette Books please write to:

Jane Nicholls
Silhouette Books
PO Box 236
Thornton Road
Croydon
Surrey CR9 3RU

One

___

Dear Aunt Miranda,

My problem may not sound very serious to you, but believe me, it's making my life miserable. I am fourteen years old and terribly shy. When I'm hanging around with the guys, I'm fine, but as soon as I see a cute girl, I just seem to clam up. I can't think of a single thing to say. I can imagine what they must think of me. Of course, under the circumstances, asking a girl for a date is out of the question. None of the other guys seem to have this problem, and I'm sure they'd laugh if I asked them for advice. You're the only one I can turn to, so please hurry with an answer.

Signed,
Fourteen and Desperate
For A Date

Dear Desperate,

The first thing you must remember is that fourteen is always a difficult age.

"Baloney!" Randy Wade muttered vehemently under her breath.

Plucking the pencil out from behind her ear, she scribbled over the words she'd typed at the top of the page. What teenage boy was going to stand for an answer like that? It was pompous, and even worse, patronizing. If he was a typical fourteen-year-old, what he wanted from her was a solid plan of action, not some vague reassurance about the future.

Frowning, Randy rolled the piece of paper down through her typewriter until she reached a clean spot to begin again. It was tempting, she knew, to wax philosophical from the vantage point of a life lived twice as long as that of the boy who had written the letter. Indeed, at the age of twenty-eight, she often felt as though she had seen and done almost everything, most of it the hard way.

Oblivious to the noise and confusion that reigned around her in the crowded back office of the small Connecticut newspaper, Randy huddled over her machine. Her fingers waited, poised uselessly over the keys as she realized she had nothing to say. Scowling down at the blank piece of paper before her, she straightened, then settled back into her oversize desk chair, tilting it on its axis.

Long auburn hair spilled down over her shoulders, and she threaded a finger through the thick strands and began to twirl them idly. Her eyes, a tawny golden shade of hazel, warmed with sympathy as she considered the boy's dilemma.

If anyone ought to be able to give good advice on how to combat insecurity, it was she, Randy mused. Indeed by now, she ought to be an expert. Her childhood, she reflected, was not the type that had been conducive to forming relationships, lasting or otherwise. Painfully withdrawn through-out those years, she herself hadn't even started dating until she'd entered college.

Thank God Desperate didn't know that, thought Randy, her features relaxing into a wry smile. He'd probably retract his letter and fire it off to Ann Landers instead!

Sitting behind her desk, Randy laughed out loud at the very idea. It had taken her a long time to find her own special niche in the world, but now that she had, competition of that sort was the least of her worries. No, after eighteen months of sure but steady success, her advice column for teenagers, "Dear Aunt Miranda" was in no danger on that score.

Indeed, Randy mused, its widespread acceptance right from the start had surprised everybody, herself included. In less than two months, the column had grown from a weekly item to a daily feature as its popularity had soared. And the reason for that popularity, she knew, was the kids. To her continuing delight, Glendale's teenage population had taken Aunt Miranda immediately to heart. Their response had been fantastic.

Her mail, a steady trickle in the beginning, was now delivered to her desk by the bagful. The questions covered everything from how to deal with drugs, to the right corsage to buy a girl for the prom. Picking and choosing carefully among them, Randy tried to cover the most representative problems—those that would apply to a variety of kids, not just the readers who had gotten up the nerve to write in.

Like this one, she thought, gazing down at the still-empty sheet sitting in the typewriter before her. Desperate's plight was a common one among teenagers. What she needed to give him was a good common-sense answer, one that offered useful ideas for overcoming the problem, while at the same time, subtly letting him know he was not alone.

Dear Desperate,

You're right, shyness can make you miserable. I should know. I, too, was very shy when I was your age. Girls may seem like a foreign species to you now, but believe me, this is only temporary.

What you really need to do right now is to meet more girls, not less. Get to know them as friends, as people, and you will find your fears vanishing. How about joining some of the after-school activities that girls tend to be involved in? Glee club or drama club might be a good place to start. Opt for home ec. instead of shop, and you'll have it made! Go to the school mixers and make yourself mingle. Try standing next to the punch bowl. Help the girls get their drinks. You don't have to dance. At this stage of the game, talking is enough.

Relax, take your time, and you'll soon be comfortable. If it makes things any easier, try to think of this as an adventure—or maybe an outing to the zoo! Even the most exotic species can turn out to be very friendly, once you get to know them.

Signed,
Aunt Miranda

Bracing her elbows on either side of her typewriter, Randy rested her chin in her palms and reread what she had written. Satisfied with her response, she rolled the paper out of the machine, clipped the letter to the top of the page, and set it in her "Out" basket. Desperate would find his answer in Friday afternoon's paper.

"Hey Randy, a bunch of us are going down to Delmonico's to get a pizza for lunch. Do you want to come?"

Randy looked up over her desk into the smiling face of Jenna Parks, the assistant editor of the women's page. "No, I don't think so." She shook her head slowly, gesturing toward the large sack of letters the mailboy had dumped beside her desk early that morning. "Even without taking a break, I've got enough work to keep me busy for hours. Besides, the team's got soccer practice this afternoon, and I was hoping to skip out a little early."

Jenna sighed, peering down into her friend's face closely. "Has it ever occurred to you, that your priorities are all out of whack? Anyone who could consciously choose running around a big green field after a little black-and-white ball, over eating hot gooey pizza, has got to be at least slightly deranged."

"I'm the coach, remember?" Randy said with a laugh. "I don't have to run around after the ball, I just have to supervise the girls while they do it. Besides," she added, glancing down meaningfully at her friend's amply padded waistline, "a little exercise never hurt anybody."

"Of course not," Jenna said back over her shoulder, having the last word as she wound her way toward the door through the maze of desks in the small room. "That's why we're walking the block and a half to Delmonico's instead of taking the car."

Chuckling, Randy reached for the mailbag at her feet. She hoisted it up onto the desk and tilted it on its end, spilling several dozen letters out onto the worn blotter. The room had quieted considerably as, one by one, her co-workers had left to go to lunch, and now she looked forward to an hour or so of relative peace in which to do her reading.

Lost in thought, Randy had no idea how much time had passed when a loud commotion in the next room summoned her attention back to the present. She jumped slightly, as the door to the outer office slammed, and glanced up as an obviously irate male voice demanded, "All right, where is she?"

Where's who? Randy wondered, startled by the man's tone. She couldn't imagine what anyone at their little newspaper could have done to elicit such an angry response. The ghost of a smile played about her lips as she remembered last week's editorial on swamp drainage. That couldn't be it. Perhaps it was the florist, whose ad on page three had inadvertently been run with the copy upside down.

Cocking her head to listen, she heard the faint sound of the receptionist's soothing tones forming a reply. Though she couldn't make out exactly what was said, it was obvious that the answer the man sought was not the one he was given, for almost immediately his voice came booming through the room again.

"I don't care what your policy on the subject is, I demand to see this woman, and right now!"

Slowly Randy's smile died. Whether he thought he had a just cause or not, that was no way to treat Bonnie, the paper's timid, eager-to-please, young receptionist. Just who did he think he was, anyway, coming in here and riding roughshod over people who were only trying to do their jobs?

Randy's chair scraped across the linoleum floor as she pushed it back from her desk. So he wanted to try his hand at intimidation, did he, she thought, rising to her full height of just under six feet. Then let him try it with someone his own size!

The first thing Randy saw when she reached the doorway was that, despite her stature, the man in the outer office still managed to top her by several inches. And not only was he tall...

Abruptly Randy's forward motion slowed then stopped altogether as she found herself confronting a giant of a man whose very presence seemed to fill the whole outer room. Quickly her eyes flickered up and down over him, and what she saw was enough to make her breath catch in her throat.

His skin was tanned to an even shade of bronze, a fact which made his blue eyes stand out all the more in a face that went beyond being conventionally handsome and approached the stuff that dreams are made of. From the strong slope of his cheekbones, to the narrow aristocratic nose, to the sharply defined angle of his jaw, his features combined in a face that was compellingly attractive, yet at the same time, vitally masculine. Dark, mahogany-brown hair glinted beneath the fluorescent lights, framing his face in a mass of tight curls.

Her assessment traveled downward, and Randy's gaze lingered appreciatively on a body that was large, but at the same time, lean and fit. As far as she could see there was not an ounce of spare flesh on him anywhere. No wonder Bonnie had been thrown by his appearance, she thought wryly. His rudeness was obviously not the man's only outstanding feature!

Pulling her eyes away, Randy sent the receptionist a reassuring glance and received a look of almost tangible relief in return. "Is there anything I can do to help?" she asked, crossing the room to stand beside the reception desk.

The question had been directed at Bonnie, but as the young woman hesitated, her hand gesturing weakly in the man's direction, he took it upon himself to answer for her.

"I certainly hope so," he growled, obviously irritated by the need to explain himself all over again. "My name is Nick Jarros, and I am here to speak to the woman who goes by the name of Aunt Miranda."

Randy gasped softly, covering the sound with a hasty clearing of her throat. So that was what the commotion had been all about! Bonnie, in her own sweet way, must have taken one look at this steamroller of a man and decided that Randy needed protecting. Her tawny eyes narrowed thoughtfully. From the looks of him, the receptionist might not have been wrong.

Throwing back her shoulders, Randy faced him squarely. "Do you have an appointment?" she asked coolly, stalling for time while she pondered what to do.

As Bonnie had undoubtedly already told him, Aunt Miranda's identity was a closely guarded secret. Indeed, no one save her handful of co-workers on the small paper's staff was privy to the person behind the name. Such a ruse was vital in maintaining her credibility among the town's teenagers, Randy reflected, knowing that if they were truly to confide their innermost doubts and fears, they must think of the columnist as an anonymous figurehead—one with whom their secrets would always be safe.

Under the circumstances, talking to Nick Jarros could prove tricky, Randy mused. Then again, in his present state of mind, sending him away might be equally difficult. It was just her luck that he should have shown up now, at lunch time, when the office was virtually empty.

Not that he actually looked dangerous, Randy decided, studying him closely. No, to all appearances, he was just very, very angry. Maybe she *should* talk to him, try and defuse that anger, and most of all, find out why it was aimed in her direction.

"No, of course I don't have an appointment!" Nick snapped in answer to her question. "If I did, I'd hardly be standing around out here wasting my time as well as yours."

As he spoke, Randy's gaze was drawn once more to his face, with its arresting features and cool, china-blue eyes. Who was she trying to kid, she wondered. With looks like those, he could be Jack the Ripper and she'd still be tempted to hear him out. No doubt about it, this man was lethal all right. But somehow she suspected that physical safety was going to be the least of her worries.

"Perhaps something can be arranged," Randy announced, hiding her misgivings behind a cool, forbidding tone. "If you would step this way..."

Spinning on her heel, she strode back across the room to the inner office. Though she didn't look to see if he was coming, Randy had taken no more than a dozen steps before she realized that it wasn't necessary. The tingling she felt at her nape was a sure indicator of his presence behind her.

Not bad, Nick thought to himself, as he followed her across the room. Not bad at all. Forgetting for a moment the purpose of his visit, he allowed himself the luxury of enjoying the view. Though as a rule his tastes ran more to petite, ultrafeminine women, for this particular redhead he might be willing to make an exception.

She might be tall, but she carried herself well, he noted, her height detracting not a bit from the easy, loose-limbed grace with which she moved. Involuntarily his gaze was drawn to the soft, subtle sway of her hips. Like everything else about her, there was nothing blatantly sexy about her walk. And yet, for some reason, he couldn't seem to take his eyes off her.

She was wearing a pair of soft cotton pants, lightly flared across the hips then tapering in at the ankles, and he found himself wondering what the legs looked like that lay beneath. Slim, he'd guess, judging from the rest of her, but muscles wouldn't surprise him either. She was not only a tall woman, but a strong one as well. He'd realized that the moment she stepped through the door to lend support to the meek young thing they had guarding the front desk.

There'd been nothing weak or retiring about the way she'd thrust out her chin and faced him squarely; no hint at all that she found him even the slightest bit intimidating. Indeed, if anything, he was the one who had been taken aback. He'd been surprised by the incongruity of her expression; the self-righteous blaze burning in the eyes that gazed at him from the lovely, clear-skinned face of a sixteenth-century madonna.

For a moment he'd been quite at a loss for words, thought Nick. A small, self-satisfied smile tugged at the corners of his mouth as he remembered the look she had given him, and he realized that the feeling must have been mutual. Just as soon as he got his business with that crazy Aunt Miranda out of the way this woman was definitely going to be next on his list....

Following her through the doorway into the back office, Nick paused abruptly. He forgot all about the woman before him, his eyes narrowing suspiciously as he gazed around the small, cluttered room. Decorated in what could only be termed a haphazard style, it was crammed to capacity with a rich assortment of desks, tables and metal file cabinets. But the most notable feature, Nick realized immediately, was that, aside from the furniture, the room was utterly empty.

He scowled as the redhead, sensing he had stopped, did the same herself and turned to face him. What the hell was she up to anyway?

"I thought I told you," he said, his voice rumbling softly like distant thunder, "I've come to see Aunt Miranda."

Determinedly Randy ignored his tone as she assumed the mantle of her charade. "Yes, I know," she said evenly, "but as you can clearly see, at the moment, there's no one else here. If you'd care to discuss your problem with me, I'll be happy to see that Aunt Miranda gets your message."

She was toying with him, Nick realized angrily. That much was obvious. Well if that was what she wanted, she'd find him only too happy to play along.

"Oh you will, will you?" he growled softly. His eyes lit with a predatory gleam as he took several steps into the room, deliberately not stopping until they stood so close together that Randy was able to feel the heat his body generated.

To her chagrin, her own response came instantly as her nerve endings began to tingle beneath his avid gaze. Instinctively, as it had in the past, the realization triggered a withdrawal. Stiffening slightly, she pulled herself away.

"Yes, of course," she managed, dismayed by the weakness her voice betrayed. "I realize you'd rather talk to Aunt Miranda in person, but I'm afraid that simply won't be possible. I'm sorry to have to disappoint you...."

"Believe me," Nick drawled, favoring her with a slow, sensuous smile. "I'm not disappointed at all."

Wonderful, thought Randy. That was just great. In one fell swoop, she managed to turn him from a bull on the rampage to a wolf on the prowl. Right this moment she wasn't at all sure which of the two she preferred.

Carefully she steered the conversation back to safer channels. "You did say there was a problem you wanted to discuss with me?"

"Not you," Nick corrected, his cobalt-blue eyes narrowing. "Aunt Miranda."

"Yes, of course," Randy stammered. "That's what I meant." Damn! How could she have allowed him to fluster her this way? At this rate, next thing she knew, she'd be handing him the keys to the company safe!

"Then perhaps you'd care to show me to your office where we can talk this out in private?"

"I don't have an office," said Randy, finding herself grateful for that deficiency for the first time in her life. No doubt about it, the last thing she needed with this man was more privacy! "I have an alcove and a desk. If you'd like to follow me, they're right over here."

She was cool, he'd give her that, thought Nick, mentally chalking up another plus on the woman's side of the scoreboard. He didn't know what the connection with that crazy Aunt Miranda was, but the gripe he'd come to air was a legitimate one. Her reasons for taking the heat in the old biddy's stead were her own business. But if she thought he was about to go easy on her because she had a cute tush... Nick frowned, irritated by the direction of his thoughts. The sooner he got this whole mess done and over with, the better. And then afterward...

"Now suppose you tell me exactly what this is all about," Randy said firmly as they reached her desk. She gestured toward the flimsy metal camp chair which sat alongside, waiting until he had lowered his bulk onto the small seat, before walking around to sit down as well.

"I'll tell you what it's about," Nick said smoothly, but with an edge to his voice that clearly revealed the presence of reawakened anger. "It's about a letter my daughter Wendy wrote to Aunt Miranda."

"Wendy, Wendy Jarros," Randy said thoughtfully, turning the name over in her mind. It sounded familiar, but she couldn't quite place it. Certainly not in connection with any letter she might have received. Frowning, she shook her head slightly. "I'm afraid I still don't know who—"

"As I understand it, she didn't sign her own name," Nick broke in impatiently. Then realizing what she had said, he peered at her closely across the desk, his brow lowering in an ominous scowl. If he didn't know better, he'd swear she was altogether too familiar in her association with this mysterious Aunt Miranda.

"Of course." Oblivious to his scrutiny, Randy relaxed slightly as her confusion faded. "Most of the kids don't. When it comes to looking for advice, anonymity is a large part of the service the column offers."

"I don't care about most kids," Nick snapped. "At the moment I'm only interested in my daughter and the problems Aunt Miranda has created for both of us."

Randy desperately wished she knew which letter it was that his daughter had sent. Without that vital piece of information she was flying blind. She was certain she hadn't done anything wrong, but how could she possibly defend herself when she wasn't even sure what the charges were?

"Wendy probably never should have written that letter to begin with, but she did. And when she read that irresponsible, sophomoric reply—"

"Now wait just a minute!" Randy cried, responding to the insult with an automatic burst of outrage.

From the moment she'd first set eyes on him, Nick Jarros had thrown her off balance. Now her response to him was so strong that, in the heat of her anger, both the charade and the common sense that had prompted it were tossed aside as though they'd never even existed.

Leaning over her desk, she glared at him across the short distance that separated them. "I'll have you know, Mr. Jarros," she said, forming the words slowly and distinctly, "there is nothing either irresponsible or sophomoric about my column—"

"Aha!" Nick roared triumphantly. He leapt to his feet, towering over her with all the satisfaction of a mongoose who has finally managed to pin down a weaving cobra. "So now it's *your* column, is it?"

"No!" Randy recanted in horror as she realized what she had said. "That isn't what I meant at all."

"Like hell!" Nick smiled knowingly. Propping his hands on the top of her desk, he leaned down over the blotter that separated them, surrounding her with his presence. "I should have guessed. I *would* have guessed, except..." He paused, his eyes moving with deliberate lack of haste over the contours of her figure. "Well, let's just say you're not at all what I expected, *Aunt Miranda*."

Clearly, there was no point in continuing to deny the obvious, Randy decided, moving quickly to take the offensive. "Don't tell me," she said sweetly, "let me guess. You had Aunt Miranda all figured out in your mind as a kindly little old lady, complete with knitting bag and broad-brimmed hat."

"Hardly," Nick retorted, determined not to let her see that at least as far as the physical description went, her guess had not been far wrong. "From what I saw of the letter you wrote to my daughter, a barracuda could handle that column of yours more kindly."

Gritting her teeth, Randy fumed her way through a silent count to ten before daring to form a reply. As far as an attempt at diplomacy went, it didn't do her the slightest bit of good.

"If you had ever read Aunt Miranda's column, Mr. Jarros, which by the way I sincerely doubt, you'd realize that it deals with the very real needs of this town's teenagers. I have no idea what I may have told your daughter, but whatever it was, I assure you the advice was given in good faith—"

"Good faith, hah!" Nick bellowed, and the desk shook beneath him. Straightening, he began to pace back and forth across the alcove. "Tell me, Aunt Miranda, do you actually consider it the act of a responsible adult to tell an impressionable teenage girl that the parental guidelines her father has set for her are nothing more than, and I quote, an outmoded set of rules left over from the middle ages?"

"Oh my God," Randy muttered softly under her breath. Now she knew who he was! The father of the girl who had written in, signing herself "A Prisoner in Glendale." If memory served her correctly, she had agreed with his daughter on every one of her complaints. And not only that, calling him outmoded was one of the kinder things she had said in her reply. In fact, she seemed to remember making some reference to rules that should have gone out with the Spanish Inquisition, and adults who had no right to assert their authority by bullying their children....

"Well?" Nick demanded. "I asked you a question, Aunt Miranda. Is that how you get your kicks, by leading astray the children who write to you for advice?"

"Certainly not!" Randy flared. "And for Pete's sake, stop calling me Aunt Miranda! My name is Randy, Randy Wade."

"I wish I could say that it's a pleasure Miss Wade, but under the circumstances..." Nick abruptly stopped pacing, his eyes lighting on the letter she had just finished typing that morning. Reaching down, he snatched it up off her desk and began to read.

"Hey!" Randy cried, leaping up and striding around her desk. "Give that back. You have no right!"

Ignoring her protests, Nick merely held the letter out of her reach as he continued to read. "Not bad," he said when he had finished. "At least you didn't blame *his* parents for everything that's gone wrong in his life since the day he entered high school!"

"I try never to lay the blame on anybody!" Randy snapped, then flushed guiltily, remembering the reply she had written his daughter. But what else was she to tell a girl who wrote in to say that her father was so overprotective that, at the age of fifteen, she was allowed neither to date, nor to talk to boys on the phone?

"So," Nick drawled, intercepting the look that flashed across her face and interpreting its meaning correctly. "I see you're finally beginning to remember."

"You're right, I am," Randy returned evenly. One thing was sure, when she'd told this man's daughter that her father was a bully, she hadn't been far off the mark at all. "And at the same time I'm also remembering that your daughter referred to herself in her letter to me as a virtual prisoner." Randy glared at him accusingly. "Really Mr. Jarros, the way she described her situation made it sound like house arrest would be a pleasant alternative."

"I'm sure she did." Nick smiled slightly, but the expression held neither warmth nor a suggestion of humor. "I assume that before you wrote your reply, it never occurred to you that teenage girls have a natural propensity for exaggeration?''

"Well..." Randy said slowly. Good Lord, she thought with a gulp, was it possible she could have been wrong in her assessment of the situation? There was only one way to find out. "Then am I to believe that the things your daughter wrote in her letter are not true? For example," Randy paused briefly, relishing the idea of putting him on the spot as he had done to her, "*is* she allowed to date?"

To his credit, Nick Jarros had the grace to look slightly discomfited. "It's not that she isn't allowed," he said huffily. "It's just that none of the boys she's brought home so far have been suitable."

Of course not, Randy thought dryly. "And she isn't allowed to talk to them on the phone either?"

Frowning, Nick uttered an impatient snort. "What good would it do her to talk to them on the phone? As far as I could tell, most of them are barely articulate anyway."

Quickly Randy bit back a smile. Obviously it had never occurred to this man just what an intimidating presence he could be. No wonder he thought his daughter's prospective suitors had nothing to say!

"And when she does go out with a group of friends, she has to be home no later than ten o'clock, even on weekends?"

"Right," Nick said shortly. "That's the rule, and I made it for her own good. I may look old to you, Miss Wade, but I remember all too well just what kinds of trouble kids her age can get into."

Old? Randy thought, her eyes skimming downward over his hard, well-toned physique. Who was he trying to kid? There was nothing about the man to even suggest that he was anything other than a very healthy male specimen in the absolute prime of his life.

Then again, she mused, with his looks, he was the type who could get away with murder where women were concerned, and probably had. Nor did he look like someone who would feel obliged to live by anybody's rules but his own. And if that were true...Randy nodded slowly. All at once, some of the reservations he had about his daughter's behavior were beginning to make perfect sense.

"Then what you're really trying to say is that if you give Wendy too much freedom, you're afraid she'll meet someone like you?"

Randy jumped as Nick slammed his hand, palm open, down on the top of her desk. "That's not what I said at all, and you know it!"

"But it *is* what you meant, isn't it?"

"It was bad enough when you only gave bad advice," Nick bit out sharply. "If I were you, I wouldn't try dabbling in psychoanalysis as well!"

"Oh for Pete's sake!" Randy snapped. "I only meant to point out—"

"Spare me, Miss Wade." Nick sighed theatrically. "I know exactly what you were trying to do. You just can't resist poking your nose in where it doesn't belong, can you?"

"Let me remind you, Mr. Jarros," Randy said furiously, adopting the same theatrical tone, "it was your daughter who wrote to me, not the other way around!"

"And I suppose you think *that* absolves you of all blame?"

Randy propped her hands on her hips angrily. Her temper was definitely getting the better of her, and she knew that was a bad sign. At the best of times, she was hardly a tactful person. With her ire up, she was all too likely to say something she'd later regret.

"If we're assigning blame around here, " she said silkily, "how about taking some for yourself? If you treated your daughter like a normal parent, showing some compassion or understanding, then she wouldn't have anything to complain about, now would she?''

"That does it!" snapped Nick. "I don't have to stand here and listen to this kind of abuse. I was hoping we might be able to discuss this problem like two mature, reasonable adults, but I can see that I'm only wasting my time!"

"I couldn't agree with you more," Randy countered as Nick turned on his heel and started away. She couldn't resist throwing one last barb at his departing back. "But if by chance the moment should ever arise when you're feeling either mature or reasonable, please feel free to come back and try it again!"

The sound of the door slamming shut in the outer office echoed through the empty room as the strength drained from her body and Randy sank slowly back down into the chair behind her desk.

Was it her imagination, she wondered, or had she actually just survived a visit from a human tornado?

Two

Dear Aunt Miranda,

Since you're a woman, I'm hoping you'll be able to answer a question for me. For the past three months, I've been going steady. In the beginning, everything was great, but now my girlfriend is starting to act as though she thinks she owns me. In fact, she's getting to be just like my mother—bossy. She nags me about everything from the color of my socks to the amount of time I spend with the guys. It's getting so that I'm afraid she's going to call me some night and remind me to brush my teeth!

So here's my question. Are all girls like this, or just the ones I've met so far (my mother and my steady)? If they are, I guess I'll just have to learn to live with it, but if they're not, please let me know fast. I can't do anything about my mother, but I sure can trade in my girl.

Sign Me,

Too Young To Be Henpecked

Sprawled out lazily over the length of her flowered damask couch, Randy giggled delightedly over the letter she held in her hand. Poor Henpecked, it sounded as though his lot in life had been destined from the start.

That thought brought fresh peals of laughter that Randy indulged shamelessly. The crumpled piece of stationery slipped from her fingers and drifted to the floor beneath the coffee table. Reaching down to retrieve it, she managed to dislodge the small stack of letters she'd brought home from the office to go through, and they cascaded down onto the rug as well.

It was par for the course, Randy thought wryly. Looking back now, it seemed as though her whole day had been one mishap after the other. That disastrous meeting with Nick Jarros was only the first incident, and to her dismay, it had set the tone for the rest of the afternoon.

Thanks to Bonnie's enthusiastic and repeated retelling of the event, it wasn't long before the whole office had been treated to a report of the irate father's visit. Between the teasing comments that had inevitably ensued and then the time she'd wasted mentally chastising herself for not handling the situation better in the first place, Randy had been unable to get any work done at all.

By four-thirty, she'd given up on the effort. Packing up a bundle of letters to read at home, she'd ducked into the ladies' room for a quick change of clothing, then driven over to the high school field where Glendale's girls' intermural soccer team was assembling for practice.

Ordinarily, coaching the team, as she'd done three times a week since its inception a month earlier, was the high point of her day. But this afternoon, even the girls' enthusiastic play had been unable to provide the balm she needed. Her timing was off, and her concentration was nonexistent. By the time she'd found herself calling the same foul for the third time in as many minutes, she felt snappish and irritable.

It didn't help matters in the slightest when she benched the players responsible, for as soon as she called the substitutes up from the sidelines, she'd realized why the name Wendy Jarros had sounded so familiar in her office that afternoon. Wendy, a slender, brown-haired girl of fifteen, was her second-string goalie.

Funny, Randy mused, sitting up to gather the letters and place them once more atop the table. She would never have associated the gregarious, outspoken girl, who handled the goalie's tricky post with such flair and aplomb, with the letter Aunt Miranda had received in the mail several weeks earlier. She didn't know Wendy well, but from what she'd seen she'd assumed the girl was capable of handling almost any sort of situation that might arise.

In that regard, Randy reflected, Wendy bore a notable resemblance to her father. No wonder the two of them didn't get along. She grinned, picturing their home life. One thing was sure—she didn't envy Mrs. Jarros one bit. Her husband might be a hunk on wheels, but with two such strong personalities under one roof the poor woman probably had all she could do just trying not to get caught in the cross fire.

Mrs. Jarros! Abruptly Randy gulped as the thought brought her up short. in all the time she'd spent talking to Nick that afternoon, it had never even once crossed her mind that he might be married. But he had to be, didn't he? Teenaged daughters like Wendy didn't spring fully formed from out of nowhere.

Pursing her lips, Randy frowned pensively. Now that she stopped and thought about it, she seemed to remember that Wendy had mentioned something in her letter about her parents being divorced. And of course, that would make sense. After all, no married man in his right mind had any business looking at another woman the way Nick Jarros had looked at her. Why, before he'd found out that she was Aunt Miranda some of those smoldering glances he'd sent in her direction would have melted a popsicle at fifty paces. Lord knew, she herself had been near enough to melting...

Randy scowled at the memory, determinedly pushing it aside. Married, single, what was the difference? Once he knew who she really was, his opinion of her couldn't have been plainer, or less complimentary. Clearly the man had no use for either her or her column.

"And speaking of your column..." Randy muttered irritably under her breath. Nick Jarros might be a devastatingly attractive man, but it was bad enough she'd already wasted her entire afternoon on his account. She was damned if she was going to waste her evening as well.

Picking up the top letter once more, Randy leaned back on the couch and began to compose her reply. As often happened, the writer's problems triggered memories of her own childhood years, and now she gave her thoughts free rein, knowing from experience that one of the things the teenagers valued about her advice was that she never tried to hide the fact that she too, had "been there."

Not, of course, that all her experiences were directly related, Randy mused. Certainly she herself had never been subjected to a nagging boyfriend. Now the mother, that was another story...

Her head nestled against the soft, plump cushions, Randy closed her eyes and let the images come. Quickly, like a stack of flash cards, displayed and then discarded, a series of faces flashed through her mind. Her mothers, all three of them.

Some more successful in their role than others, but all with one thing in common. They couldn't quite figure out what to make of the shy, withdrawn child the welfare board had placed in their care.

Orphaned at the age of four, Randy had first been placed in the care of her aunt, a harried divorcee who, with three children of her own, had neither the time, nor the inclination to add another. Her strongest recollections of those early years were of there never seeming to be enough to go around. From clothing to affection, everything she'd been grudgingly given had been secondhand.

When her aunt had remarried two years later, the problem had only intensified. Her new stepfather was a widower with two teenage children of his own; and in the large, noisy household that ensued, Randy had felt like more of an outsider than ever. She had withdrawn into her own private world, weaving childish fantasies about the parents she could barely remember.

It was at least partly her fault, Randy knew, that her stepparents had never seemed to know what to do with her. And with five other children all clamoring for attention, they had no time to try to understand—to break through the quiet, introspective facade she hid behind so well. Instead it had been only a matter of months before they convinced themselves that what she really needed was professional attention. Reassuring each other that what they were doing was for the best, they had packed her tiny suitcase, kissed her on the cheek, and delivered her over to the social services.

The next few years blurred together in a series of encounters, some brief, some longer, as she was passed from one foster home to another under the care of the welfare board. Some were undeniably better than others, but by then it was simply too late. Randy had already isolated herself behind a prickly wall of impenetrable reserve. Eventually even the most determined of guardians had been forced to give up, labeling her difficult and unresponsive.

She attended half a dozen schools in as many years, never remaining in one place long enough to form the friendships she so desperately craved, and never having the chance to experience what it was like to have a place where she truly belonged. By the time Randy reached her early teens, the patterns of her life had been firmly set. She went to school, did her chores and kept mostly to herself.

She was old enough now to be useful in her foster homes, and that in itself earned her a measure of appreciation. Randy didn't mind the work, indeed she welcomed it. Serving as companion for two younger children, she had stayed with one family for nearly a year, and had almost begun to believe that this time things might actually work out.

Soon after her fourteenth birthday however, all that had changed. At first when her foster father began paying more attention to her, she had assumed that he was merely grateful for the little extra things she tried to do around the house to make their life more comfortable. It had therefore come as quite a shock when she'd been confronted by her foster mother, and accused, in no uncertain terms, of leading the man on.

Until that moment, Randy had paid no more attention to her looks than she had to any of the other, myriad, details of her life that she couldn't change. She knew she was tall for her age: she'd always been. And thanks to the jeering taunts of the boys at school, she couldn't help but be aware that her body had begun to fill out in what could only be termed a rather amazing way. Still, she'd never flaunted herself; indeed if anything, the opposite was true, as she tried to hide her emerging figure under baggy tops of various shapes and sizes.

Randy's tearful denials had gone for nothing however. Within a month, she had found herself placed once more on the roster of homeless children. After that, placements had become more and more difficult to find. Throughout her teenage years, Randy had felt as though she was simply marking time, waiting for the days to pass until at the age of eighteen, armed with only a high-school diploma and a clear idea of the sort of life she wanted to build for herself, she had set out to make it on her own.

Working days and studying nights, she'd managed to put herself finally through college. After that, she drifted through a variety of jobs, knowing deep down inside what she was seeking, but somehow not quite able to find it. A stint working as copy girl on one of the large daily newspapers in New York had begun to clarify those goals. More classes, this time in journalism, had followed. But is wasn't until Randy had left the city, finding herself inexorably drawn to the homey small-town atmosphere of Glendale, a tiny hamlet in northwest Connecticut, that she knew she had begun to find her niche.

And now, thought Randy, she finally had almost everything she ever wanted—a cosy home of her own, a circle of friends among her co-workers at the paper and two jobs— one as Aunt Miranda and the other as coach—that she found immensely rewarding. For the first time there was a sense of real stability in her life—a stability that for years she had only dreamed of. It was, Randy reflected, a wonderful feeling.

Smiling at the thought, she turned her attention back to the letter which lay forgotten in her hand. Skimming through it again, she realized she couldn't help but agree with the boy's own assessment of the situation, as reflected by the signature he had chosen.

Nodding to herself, Randy snatched up a pencil and began to scribble her reply.

Dear Henpecked,

   If your mother and your girlfriend are the only girls you know, then you definitely *are* too young, not only to be nagged at all the time, but to be going steady as well. Why tie yourself down at such an early age? There are millions of girls in the world you haven't even met yet. And no, in answer to your question, they are not all bossy. If I were you, I'd forget about going steady for the time being, and set about having a variety of different experiences. You're only going to be young once, you know. Take the opportunity and enjoy it while you can!

                              Signed,
                              Aunt Miranda
P.S. What color are those socks of yours anyway?

   The following afternoon Randy got held up at her desk making last-minute adjustments to the next day's column. By the time she dashed into the ladies' room to change and discovered that the red striped nylon running shorts she'd packed to wear that afternoon had shrunk in the wash, she was already late for soccer practice.

   "Damn!" Randy swore softly, studying her reflection ruefully in the full length mirror. At her height, it was hard enough finding clothes that fit. And these shorts *had* fit, apparently until just the other night when she'd thrown them in the laundry for the first time. Now however, they barely covered her buttocks, much less the tops of her thighs.

   Quickly Randy untucked the roomy, white cotton tee shirt she was wearing on top. Just as quickly, she decided that that wouldn't do at all. Though its long tails added at least an inch to the coverage she achieved, the new outfit now had the unfortunate effect of looking as though she wasn't wearing any shorts at all!

"Oh, for Pete's sake!" Randy muttered, shoving the long hem back into her shorts. She'd just have to make do. What difference did it make anyway? It was a sure bet that the twenty some teenaged girls on her team couldn't care less how much thigh she exposed. And as for their boyfriends who sometimes came to line the sidelines of the field? Randy shrugged. If she had to take some good-natured ribbing from that quarter, she was mature enough to handle it.

From the newspaper office, which was housed in a quaint Victorian home on the main street of town, it took less than ten minutes to reach the high school playing field. As she pulled into the lot, Randy could see that the team was not only already assembled but had, in her absence, begun to run some drills.

Climbing from her car, she took a moment to catch her breath, pausing and inhaling deeply of the rich, fragrant summer air. Though New England was renowned for its other seasons—cold, blustery winters, verdant springs and brilliantly colored autumns—this was the time of year she liked the best, when the days were drowsily warm and sunlight lasted long into the night.

"Hey Randy, come on, hurry up, you're late! Three laps around the field, remember?"

Looking over to where the team had stopped their drill to wait for her, Randy grinned. No doubt about it, her girls didn't believe in pulling any punches. Flipping her long auburn braid back over her shoulder out of the way, she hurried out across the field to greet them.

By the time the session ended ninety minutes later, Randy was hot, sweaty, and flushed with exhilaration. After a scant month of practicing together, the team was finally beginning to play together as a cohesive unit. With their first game—in which they were set to face an intermural team from a neighboring town—less than a week away, it was definitely cause for celebration.

"Okay, everybody dismissed!" Randy announced, clapping her hands together loudly. Her gaze ran quickly over the assemblage of faces, stopping briefly to make eye contact with each one. "You did great today, all of you. Those New Milford girls better be on their toes, or we're really going to give them something to think about!"

Chattering and giggling together, the team headed back to the sidelines, with Randy following along behind. The regular assortment of parents and boyfriends were waiting to drive the girls home and, as usual, Randy hung back, waiting to make sure that everybody had a ride before leaving herself.

"Wooee, would you get a load of that!"

Kate Burnett, the team's center forward sighed, and the rest of the girls turned to look as a sleek, red Ferrari pulled into one of the slots beside the field. "Talk about a hot ticket!"

Absently Randy watched with them as the door of the low-slung car swung open. Then her eyes widened in startled amazement. Nick Jarros, her nemesis from the previous afternoon, climbed out. She stood as if rooted, her eyes skimming over him with unwilling fascination.

He was dressed much the same way as he had been the day before—in a pair of tight, well washed jeans, and an equally faded denim workshirt. Its cuffs had been rolled back to the elbows, while the collar gaped with casual insouciance at his throat. The slight breeze caught and ruffled his dark-brown curls as he paused beside the shiny red hood, surveying the field from behind a pair of mirrored aviator shades.

Randy watched as his gaze slid over the group assembled on the field. All at once his casual perusal stopped. He straightened to stand at attention, his eyes gliding back to where she stood. Even with the sunglasses, she could tell from his expression that he was every bit as surprised to see her as she was to see him. And if the scowl that marred his perfect features was anything to go by, he wasn't pleased about it either.

Defiantly Randy stood her ground, returning his glare with one of her own. So he hadn't expected to find her there. So what. She had every bit as much right to be at the high school as he did, maybe even more.

That her bravado was little more than a surface illusion became painfully apparent, however, when Randy realized that in an automatic move dictated by long years of habit, she had brought up her arms and crossed them self-consciously over her breasts, hiding them from his gaze. Frowning irritably at her own response, she slowly let her arms drop back to her sides. Though behind dark glasses to be sure, his gaze did not seem to flicker.

Good, thought Randy. He was every bit as uninterested in her as she was in him. Now if only he would maintain that attitude until she had the time to get to her car and drive away, they would be able to get through their second encounter without the trouble that had marred their first.

"Hot ticket is right!" Another girl breathed in a hushed tone, and a flurry of girlish giggles broke out around them.

"It's no big deal," Wendy Jarros said quickly. She began to jog on ahead across the field to where her father was waiting. "It's only my dad's new car."

"Oh yeah?" Kate returned lightly. "Who said I was talking about the car?"

Oblivious to the flurry of teenaged adulation he'd provoked, Nick leaned back against the still-warm hood of the Ferrari, frowning as he looked out over the field. That Aunt Miranda woman again! What the hell was she doing here? It was bad enough that she extended any influence on his daughter through her column in the paper. He had no idea they were seeing each other in person as well.

Sure, he'd listened while Wendy had babbled on enthusiastically about Randy, her soccer coach. But now he realized that he couldn't have been listening closely enough, because for some reason he'd always blithely assumed that the Randy she was referring to was a man. Of course, that was an honest mistake. After all, what the hell did a woman know about coaching sports anyway?

With the irresistible attraction of a moth winging its way toward a dangerous flame, Nick found his eyes drawn to her legs. Between the hem of her skimpy shorts and the tops of her low white sneakers ran a good yard and a half of the most gorgeous female equipment ever accorded to mankind.

And he ought to know, thought Nick. Over the years, he'd certainly spent his share of time studying the issue. Though he detested the title "leg-man" he'd never been able to dispute its suitability. And undeniably, this lady's legs were something else: long, slender, with the molding of subtly defined muscles to shape the honey-tanned calves and thighs. No doubt about it, yesterday's preview when she'd been wearing long pants, hadn't even begun to hint at the delights that lay beneath....

Then all at once, he frowned as, with the thought of yesterday's meeting, he remembered who she was. Aunt Miranda—the woman who'd managed to become the bane of his existence since he'd first heard of her only three days earlier. The way his daughter went around quoting her dictums, as though the columnist was some sort of guru, made it seem like years, rather than days.

He recalled how the interview in her office had turned out, and the frown turned into a full-fledged scowl. At the time he'd been so angry that he'd been out of the building and halfway down the block before he'd realized that not only had she not agreed to print a retraction in the paper, she hadn't even had the common decency to apologize to him! And to top it off, here she was turning up again. Well he'd be damned if this time she'd get off so easily.

"Hey dad, great! You're right on time. Too bad you didn't get here a few minutes earlier though. You would have had a chance to see me in action!" With typical teen-age exhuberance, Wendy launched herself into her father's arms for a quick hug.

"I'm sorry I missed it," Nick replied, reaching down to ruffle his daughter's hair affectionately. "Maybe next time, hmm?"

"Gee, I don't know." Wendy brushed past him to throw her gym bag into the space behind the front seat of the red sports car. "I'm only the second string goalie, not the starter, so I don't get to play all the time."

"Second string?" Nick repeated, his eyes narrowing. "How did that happen?"

Wendy shrugged. "I guess I wasn't having too good a day at the tryouts, and Patty Brach is really pretty good—"

"Nonsense," said Nick. "You're pretty good too. After all, I taught you how to handle a ball myself, didn't I?"

"Well yes, but—"

"No buts about it." Nick said firmly.

Second string indeed! he thought, fuming. If that wasn't just the last straw. Who did that woman think she was any-way, first implying that he wasn't doing a good job of rais-ing his daughter, and now all but saying that Wendy wasn't a good enough player to make the starting team? Ob-viously the woman wouldn't recognize talent if it came up and hit her over the head!

He gestured toward the car behind them. "Wait here for me a moment, will you Wendy? I just want to have a few words with your coach."

"But dad—"

"Don't worry," Nick called back over his shoulder as he took off his dark glasses and tucked them purposefully into his breast pocket. "I'll be right back."

Uh-oh, thought Randy, watching as Nick made his way across the field. Much as she wanted to believe that he had other business in the vicinity, it didn't seem likely. She sighed quietly as he came to a stop before her, his feet braced wide apart in a stance that could only be termed belligerent. So much for wishful thinking.

"Can I do something for you?" Randy asked, arching one eyebrow coolly. "Or are you just passing through?"

"Don't be cute," Nick snapped, then frowned at his own choice of words. She *was* cute dammit, that was exactly the problem. The closer he'd gotten, the better she looked. Those million-dollar legs of hers weren't helping matters one bit! How on earth could he be expected to concentrate on what he wanted to say with those on display?

Nick uttered a low, frustrated growl.

Randy's answering grin was a deliberate taunt. "Is that so?" she said, shaking her head. "I hate to mention this, but we seem to be regressing. Yesterday, you may not have made much sense, but at least you were articulate."

"Yesterday you were dressed!" Nick snapped.

Randy was taken aback. "In case you haven't noticed," she retorted, "I'm dressed now."

"More or less," Nick drawled irritably, "with the emphasis on less!" His eyes skimmed down over her once more. The least the woman could have done was have the decency to look like someone named Aunt Miranda should—old, fat, and frumpy!

"Oh for Pete's sake!" Randy said with a scowl. "Surely you didn't come all the way out here across the field just to object to my physical attributes?"

To her surprise, Nick's eyes glittered with unexpected warmth. "Believe me, Miss Wade," he said softly, his voice humming with a throaty undercurrent that seemed to stroke her senses like a velvet glove. "It's not your body I find objectionable by any means—"

"I'll just bet," Randy muttered, bracing herself resignedly for what was to follow. No doubt he was building up to one of those moronic comments about her bra size that men invariably seemed to find so witty.

"Although the packaging job you've done is another story..."

Randy looked up in surprise. Her mouth dropped open, then snapped shut.

"Don't you realize that these girls you're coaching are highly impressionable young women? You, of all people, should be trying to set a good example, *Aunt Miranda*."

"Don't call me that here," Randy hissed. She glanced around quickly, hoping they hadn't been overheard. To her relief, the team had already dispersed into small, chattering groups on the sidelines.

"Oh yes, I forgot. Nobody's supposed to be able to figure that out." Nick smiled mirthlessly. "Any more than they can figure out how somebody as obviously inept as you are got to be coach of this soccer team."

"Ooooh!" Randy bit out from between clenched teeth. "I'll have you know I work my tail off—"

"I imagine you'd have to," Nick interrupted dryly, "just to keep up at all. It's obvious you have no natural talent for the job. Why from what my daughter, Wendy, told me, I'm not even sure you've got the positions assigned right—"

Randy gasped indignantly. Who did he think he was anyway, Pele? She might not know everything about soccer, but one thing she did know. She'd heard just about all she intended to from Mr. Nick Know-It-All Jarros!

"I'll tell you what," she proposed, her voice dripping with saccharine sweetness. "If you have any more objections, why don't you sit down, write them all out...and fire off a letter to the editor!"

Before Nick had a chance to reply, Randy had brushed defiantly past him, striding away toward the lot where her car was waiting. Damn, he thought, staring after her departing back. She'd done it to him again. Now that was two apologies she owed him!

Three

Dear Aunt Miranda,

A few months ago, I did something stupid and now I really regret it. At the time I was going out with a girl named Ann, and things were pretty serious between us. Well one night I was out getting rowdy, you know, with the guys. They were razzing me about my relationship with Ann, and the next thing you know I somehow ended up with her name tattooed on a rather sensitive portion of my anatomy!

The next day we all had a good laugh about it, and of course I joined in, but I was the one stuck with the tattoo. Not only was Ann not very impressed by this symbol of my devotion, it turns out that in the meantime we've broken up.

Aunt Miranda, you've got to help me. It was bad enough having her name etched indelibly on my posterior when we were a pair, now it's going to be impossible! What am I going to tell my next girlfriend? At best, she's not going to be very pleased. At worst, she might want equal billing! At this rate, I could wind up looking like a walking billboard!

I've got to do something, and quick! Please let me know what you advise.

Yours Truly,
Signed For and Sorry

"Hey Dad, listen to this. What a hoot!" Grinning gleefully, Wendy Jarros spread the newspaper out across the breakfast table, as she read the letter aloud to her father. "Can you believe it?" she chortled when she'd finished reading. "I can't imagine who would do anything so dumb!"

"Oh, I don't know." Nick looked up over the top of the *Wall Street Journal* he was scanning. "Over the ages, men have been known to do far more foolish things than that in the name of true love."

"Oh pleeease," Wendy groaned, then her eyes brightened. "Is that the voice of experience I hear?" she asked mischievously. "Don't tell me you were ever tempted to try something like that?"

"Who me?" said Nick. Frowning, he flipped the corner of the paper back up into place, erecting a barrier between them. The last thing he needed was for his daughter to find out about some of the stunts he'd pulled in his tempestuous youth. He had enough trouble keeping her in line as it was. "Of course not."

"Sure," Wendy muttered skeptically. She picked up her spoon and went back to eating her cereal. "That's why there's that picture of you sitting on a motorcycle in your high-school year book. You know which one I'm talking about—the one with the caption underneath that reads 'Born to be Wild'?''

Abruptly the *Wall Street Journal* landed on the table in an untidy heap, rattling the coffee in Nick's cup and spilling some out onto the saucer. ''Where did you see that?'' he asked, gazing at his daughter across the table.

Wendy shrugged. ''I told you, it's right there in your high-school yearbook. What's the big deal?''

''I'm just surprised, that's all,'' said Nick, his blue eyes pensive. ''I haven't seen that old yearbook of mine in ages.''

''It's right upstairs in the attic. I found it in a box of old junk when I was looking for...'' Wendy paused, her expression suddenly clouding over.

''Looking for what?'' Nick prompted curiously.

''You know,'' said Wendy, looking somewhat embarrassed, ''a picture of mom. It's just that it's been so long since we've seen her...''

Gazing at his only child, Nick felt a swift stab of anger. In the dozen years he'd been divorced from June, he'd done his best to help Wendy adjust to life with a single parent. At times he'd even dared hope that his efforts had been successful. But each time his ex-wife forgot another birthday or settled for sending a card, rather than visiting on holidays, he saw the price that his own reckless behaviour had exacted from his daughter. It just wasn't fair! he railed inwardly, aching with frustration at the pain and anguish that brief, tempestuous marriage had caused.

When he spoke, however, his voice was soft, betraying none of the turmoil he felt inside. ''You know your mother loves you,'' he said, reaching across the table to take Wendy's hand in his. ''And I'm sure she thinks about you all the time. It's just that she's a very busy woman now, and she doesn't always have the time to keep in touch the way she'd like to.''

"No problem," Wendy said quickly. She sensed her father's need for reassurance and filled it instinctively. "I know she's got a lot on her mind these days. It doesn't bother me at all. Really."

"You're sure?" Nick asked, giving his daughter's fingers one last squeeze before drawing his hand away.

"Positive." Wendy nodded. "Besides, I only wanted the picture because we're studying genetics in biology. The teacher asked us which of our parents we resembled most and when my turn came I wasn't sure, that's all."

"I see," said Nick, but his eyes had begun to flicker with a teasing glint his daughter recognized all too well. "In that case, you go back and tell your teacher that without a doubt you inherited those brains of yours from your father's side of the family."

"Only the brains?" Wendy asked lightly, playing along.

Grinning, Nick preened for his daughter's benefit, turning his head first one way, then the other, so that she might admire his profile. "Well of course it's *obvious* where the good looks came from."

"Of course," Wendy agreed solemnly. "I knew that just as soon as I saw that picture of you on that bike. What a hunk you must have been!"

"A hunk?" Nick's eyebrows lifted as he raised his coffee cup to his lips and took a cautious sip. "Is that any way to refer to your own father?"

"It is if he looks like that," Wendy replied. Cocking her head to one side, she studied Nick judiciously. "You know, come to think of it, you still don't look so bad, even now."

"Even now?" Nick choked on a sip of coffee. "I'll have you know," he said with dignity, "I am hardly in my dotage."

"You could have fooled me," Wendy muttered, just loud enough so that her father would be sure to hear. She was hoping he would go for the bait, and he did.

"And just what exactly is that supposed to mean?"

"Oh I don't know," Wendy said casually. "I just think it's surprising that for a man your age you sure don't seem to have much interest in women."

For the second time in as many minutes, Nick choked on the hot brew. Frowning, he returned the cup to the saucer with a loud thump. "What makes you say that?"

"Well, for one thing, you hardly ever go out on dates."

Nick faced his daughter squarely across the table. "I wasn't aware you were keeping track of my social calendar."

"That's precisely the problem," Wendy pointed out calmly. "There's so little to it, it doesn't need keeping track of at all."

"You sound disappointed," Nick said incredulously, thinking of all the opportunities he had let slip by so that his daughter would know what a stable home life was—so that she would know she could always depend on him to be there for her. "Don't tell me you'd prefer it if I were out every night, galavanting around town, and staying away till all hours?"

"Of course not. But that doesn't mean I don't think you aren't entitled to any good times."

"I have plenty of good times," said Nick, his voice holding the firm ring of finality, "staying right here at home with you."

Terrific, thought Wendy, biting back a small frown. Another dead end. She'd known all along that if she was going to get her father to loosen the restrictions he'd placed on her, she was first going to have to get him to loosen the ones he'd placed on himself. But this line of reasoning didn't seem to be getting her anywhere. Maybe if she tried another tack...

"You know," she said casually, "I watched you talking to Randy the other day when you picked me up at soccer practice, and I know for a fact that she isn't married...."

"What's that got to do with anything?" Nick asked, glancing up quickly. He'd seen that speculative glint in his daughter's eye before, Nick mused, and as he recalled, he'd usually lived to regret it. Just what kind of scheme was she hatching now?

"Well it seemed to me like the two of you were getting along pretty well." Wendy paused, then added wistfully, "I mean, she is awfully pretty."

Nick growled something unintelligible under his breath.

"Well?" Wendy prodded. "Don't you think so?"

Involuntarily Nick frowned. Pretty wasn't the half of it. She'd caught his eye immediately that morning at the newspaper office; and then when he'd seen her half dressed in those skimpy shorts on the playing field...He swallowed. The woman was attractive all right.

And that wasn't all, thought Nick, remembering how she'd faced him with spirit that equaled his own. Not many women had the courage to stand up to him when he was rolling along full throttle. She'd done it not once, but twice. For that reason alone, she had him intrigued.

But that didn't mean that he could forget everything else, Nick mused. For part and parcel of that intriguing package had turned out to be the stubborn, opinionated trouble maker known as Aunt Miranda. He knew all about women like her—always sticking their noses in where they didn't belong. He should know, Nick thought grimly; his ex-wife had been one of them. That was one mistake he had no intention of repeating.

Glancing up, Nick realized that Wendy was still waiting for his reply. "I suppose she's not bad looking," he said carefully, adding an indifferent shrug for further insurance.

"Not bad?" Wendy shrieked. Now she knew it had been too long since her father had been involved with a woman. "Why she's fab-u-lous!"

Responding to his daughter's exuberant enthusiasm, Nick found he couldn't help but smile. "Is that so? And just what is it about that coach of yours that makes her so terrific?"

"You know," said Wendy, as though it was the most obvious thing in the world. Her father might be old, but he wasn't dead! Surely he must have noticed for himself. "For starters, she has a great figure, not to mention all that gorgeous red hair."

"Is that all?" Nick asked with an indulgent chuckle.

"Of course not," Wendy said quickly. "She's really smart, and she's got a great sense of humor too."

"You make her sound like a regular paragon of virtue," Nick muttered. Suddenly it was becoming all too clear just where Wendy hoped this conversation was heading.

So she thought that he ought to be interested in the charms of the inimitable Aunt Miranda, did she? Well that only went to prove what he had known all along—he was right to be wary about his daughter's judgment of the opposite sex! As far as he was concerned, the two encounters they'd already shared were plenty—enough time for him to realize just how attracted he really was, and enough for him to realize how much of a mistake that attraction could be.

"So what do you think?" asked Wendy, breaking into his thoughts. "Isn't that a great idea?"

Abruptly Nick realized he'd missed something in the conversation, something vital, judging from the expectant look on his daughter's face. "Isn't what a great idea?" he asked cautiously.

Wendy glared at him balefully. "Why you and Randy, of course! I think you'd make a super pair. I was going to get a ride home from practice with Patty tomorrow, but if you like, you can come by and pick me up instead. Then you and she can have a chance to talk—"

"Now hold on just one minute!" cried Nick, stopping the flow of words the only way he could. "What makes you think she and I have anything to talk about?"

"Well of course you do," said Wendy, sounding, Nick decided, as though she was lecturing a backward child. "Besides, how are you going to ask her out on a date if you don't talk?"

Nick's eyebrows shot up in startled surprise. "Who said anything about asking her for a date?"

Wendy groaned with exasperation. "Dad!" she wailed, "haven't you been listening to a word I said?"

"Well of course, but—"

"And after all, you did agree with me that Randy was very pretty."

"Well yes, but—"

"And you did say that it was high time you found yourself a nice woman and started having some fun."

"No," Nick broke in determinedly, glowering at his daughter across the table. "*You* said it was high time that I found a nice woman and started having some fun."

"But you agreed."

"Wendy..." Nick intoned warningly.

Wendy frowned. Somehow this wasn't going at all the way she'd hoped. "Well you didn't disagree!" she pointed out defensively.

"Now you listen here, young lady." Nick paused, until he was sure he had his daughter's undivided attention. "When and if I decide to start dating someone, *I* will be the one who decides who the lady in question is going to be. Am I making myself clear?"

"Yes daddy," Wendy sighed, favoring him with a meek smile.

Nick frowned in return, his eyes narrowing suspiciously. "Why is it I feel better when you're arguing with me than when you adopt that injured tone of yours and give in too easily?''

Wendy shrugged. "Maybe you have a guilty conscience," she suggested innocently.

"I," Nick replied with dignity "have nothing to feel guilty about."

"Well if you call browbeating your only daughter into submission nothing..." Wendy shook her head sadly. "You know Aunt Miranda says—"

"Not her again!" Nick groaned. "Can't we ever talk about anything else?"

Wendy threw up her hands in exasperation. "We just *were* talking about something else," she pointed out with asperity, "and you didn't like that topic either!"

Gazing into his daughter's guileless eyes, Nick repented as he always did. There was no doubt that his daughter had him wrapped around her little finger. The only saving grace to the situation was that she didn't seem to have realized it yet. "You're right," he said. "And I'm sorry. I didn't mean to snap at you. I know you kids think that that Aunt Miranda woman is the next best thing to the Beatles."

"The Beatles?" Wendy grimaced. "Oh daddy, you are so passé."

"I am, am I? And here I thought you said a minute ago that I wasn't so bad at all."

"Not exactly," Wendy pointed out to him teasingly. "What I said was you weren't so bad for an older man."

"For an older man," Nick echoed weakly. "Of course."

All at once it seemed as though he felt each and every one of his thirty-six years. No matter how hard they tried to bridge it, there was still that gap that loomed between them, that barrier of age and experience just large enough to prevent them from being able to fully understand each other. Nick sighed softly. Oh well, he'd just have to keep on trying. After all, what alternative was there?

"Okay," he said, smiling resignedly. "I'm listening. Tell me what Aunt Miranda has to say for herself today."

"Sure. Just a sec."

Well, thought Wendy, glancing down to locate Aunt Miranda's column in the paper before her, that hadn't gone too badly at all. Maybe there was still hope for his social life—and hers—yet. All it was going to require was a little planning on her part. And in the meantime...

Looking up with a quick smile, Wendy began to read.

Dear Signed For,

You have gotten yourself into a mess, haven't you? Maybe you'll get lucky and the next girl you fall for will be named Franny or Dianne. Then you'll only have to add on a couple of letters to keep them happy!

In case you have a more permanent solution in mind however, I did ask around, and have been informed that a tattoo can be removed. As I understand it, it is a painful and time-consuming procedure, but it may well be the answer to your prayers. The next step is to make an appointment with your dermatologist, and he will tell you where to go from there.

I know it doesn't sound great, but try to look on the bright side. Your girlfriend's name might have been Stephanie or Rosalinda. Then you'd have really been in trouble! Good luck with the removal!

Signed,
Aunt Miranda

The rest of the week seemed to fly by as Randy spent her days tending to the needs of her flourishing column, and her evenings at the extra practice sessions she had called in preparation for her fledgling soccer team's first intermural game.

After that second, disastrous encounter on the playing field, she had not run into Nick Jarros again, and Randy couldn't help but be relieved. To her chagrin however, she discovered that although the man might not be present in her life, he was never far from her thoughts.

What was it about him that managed to fascinate her so, she wondered. It was Friday afternoon and she was driving along the quiet country roads to the neighboring town of New Milford, where the game was to be held. So far, the dealings they'd had with each other had been anything but pleasant, and yet, despite the way they seemed to hiss and snap at each other on sight, she could not seem to put the formidable Mr. Jarros out of her mind.

Was it becuase he was so damnably good-looking? Randy mused. Certainly that was part of the man's appeal, but she knew herself better than to think that was all there was to it. No, she had known her share of good-looking men in the past, but none of them had managed to elicit the gut-wrenching reaction she felt whenever Nick was near.

Despite their differences, she found she couldn't help but admire him. Though the two of them might not agree on the proper way to raise a teenage daughter, it was clear from the conversations they'd had, that they both had the girl's best interests at heart. Nick might be a stern authoritarian, but he was definitely a strong and caring presence in his daughter's life. From her own experience, she knew just how precious those qualities could be.

Arriving in New Milford, Randy managed to locate the high school with little problem. As she pulled into the lot, she saw it was filling rapidly with fans, mostly boyfriends and mothers, who had turned out in honor of the first game of the summer season.

Would Nick be there too, Randy wondered, then quickly put the thought from her mind. So what if he was? He'd already made it perfectly clear by his caustic remarks, that the attraction she felt was purely one sided. Besides, she decided, climbing from her car, she had plenty of better things to do than go mooning around over some man who hadn't shown even the slightest interest in her. Things like winning this game!

The sidelines of the field were thronged with people, and Randy strode through the crowd to where her team had gathered into a noisy, animated group. Drawing near, she saw they were dressed, for the first time, in their brand new blue-and-white uniforms. Donated by a local pizza parlor, they were emblazoned with the team name, Glendale Tigers, on the back, and the slogan "Eat Manero's Pizza, it's the best!" on the front.

Randy chuckled under her breath, as she realized that the numbers on the backs of the girls' jerseys were enclosed by a large round symbol that bore a rather suspicious resemblance to a giant pizza pie. Good old Benny Manero, who was sponsoring the team, was certainly getting his money's worth!

Then again, she mused, it wasn't as though finding a patron had been easy. And after all, beggars couldn't afford to be choosers. She'd be seeing Benny that night—he'd been kind enough to offer the team a post-game dinner at the pizza parlor—and she'd have to remember to thank him again for his generosity.

"Well team, how do you feel?" she called out gaily. Her gaze flickered over the sea of eager faces that immediately turned her way. "Are you all set for the big game?"

A collection of rousing cheers answered her question resoundingly. Buoyed by their irrepressible enthusiasm, Randy took her place at the head of the group and began to lead the girls in a series of warm-up exercises. Twenty minutes later they were ready to play, and she watched with a trace of almost maternal pride as the team filed out onto the field to take up their positions.

"Come on girls, you can do it!" she yelled encouragingly, punching her upraised fist in the air. "Let's show those New Milford Maulers how the game is played!"

The group that trouped into Manero's Pizza Shack that evening for a victory dinner, was a noisy, boisterous bunch.

How on earth do I ever get myself into these things? Nick wondered, feeling decidedly out of place amid the horde of laughing teenagers. When Wendy had first enlisted his aid, insisting that, as a team father and the owner of a jeep, it was his duty to help with the transportation, he'd never imagined anything like this!

Between the members of the team, and an assortment of friends and admirers who had turned out to help them celebrate, the pizza parlor was almost crammed to capacity. Nick's gaze roamed over the room disparagingly. He supposed he should have realized that any girls' team was bound to have a following of boys, but this bunch was about as motley a crew as he'd ever seen.

In his day, boys had rebelled against authority by letting their hair grow long. How innocuous that seemed, compared to the outlandish displays he was seeing now. Anything and everything from heavily lacquered hairdos to dangling earrings were paraded about with a macho strut by youths who were barely old enough to shave. Nick scowled irritably. He'd be damned if his daughter was going to date any young man who had the audacity to poke holes in his ears.

"Hey dad, don't just stand there, come and join us!" Wendy cried. Coming up beside him, she grabbed her father's arm and ushered him forward into the room. "There's plenty of room at our table."

"Actually," Nick said quickly, "I wasn't planning on staying. How about if I head home for an hour or two while you eat? Then, when you're ready to go, you can give me a call, and I'll come down and pick everybody up?"

"Oh but you can't!" Wendy cried immediately. "Please stay, daddy. We've already ordered the pizza, and there's plenty for you. Besides, after that trip out to New Milford and back, I should think you'd be hungry." Her voice took on a solicitous tone. "Wouldn't you rather stay here and have a hot dinner than go home all alone to an empty house?"

"Well..." Nick shook his head slightly. At times, it seemed as though his daughter found him almost embarrassingly easy to get around.

Swallowing a small, resigned sigh, Nick allowed himself to be led unprotestingly to a large round table in the corner of the back room. It wasn't until they were almost there that he saw who the rest of his dinner companions were going to be. By then, it was too late.

"Look everybody!" Wendy enthused. "I found him!"

Immediately all eyes turned in their direction and Nick found himself the object of curious stares from half a dozen teenagers and a startled glance from one, very surprised looking coach. Seeing the expression on Randy's face, he couldn't help but smile. Obviously she was surprised to see him. Pursing his lips, Nick turned to regard his daughter suspiciously. What was she up to now? Why, if he didn't know better, he'd swear this whole thing had been a setup right from the start...

Quickly Wendy performed the introductions before ushering her father into one of the two empty seats. "Daddy, you remember Randy Wade, don't you? Here, why don't you take the seat right next to her?" Wendy smiled innocently. "I'm sure you two will find plenty to talk about."

"I'm sure we will," Randy muttered under her breath, edging her chair as far away as possible. Well at least that much was true—finding something to talk about had never been their problem. Now finding something to talk about civilly, that was another matter.

It really was a shame that he was so good-looking, Randy thought irritably, watching as he maneuvered his tall body down into the small wooden chair. Because aside from that, the man was an absolute menace! He seemed to take great pleasure in putting her down, while she, for her part, couldn't resist the impulse to goad him in kind. If tonight was anything like their last two meetings, this victory celebration could take on all the earmarks of World War III!

"Well," said Nick, glancing in her direction, "this is an unexpected…" His voice trailed away weakly as he tried to think of a proper end to his sentence.

"Pleasure?" Randy supplied sweetly.

"Surprise," Nick corrected, nodding to himself.

"Oh?" Randy's eyebrows lifted. So that was the way they were going to play things, were they? "I can't imagine why. After all, you saw for yourself the other day that I was the coach of your daughter's soccer team. I'd think it only a natural assumption that I might accompany them to their victory dinner."

"Yes, I suppose you're right," said Nick. Reaching for a glass of cold water, he sipped at its contents thoughtfully.

Damn, but this woman had the strangest effect on him! After all the trouble she'd caused in his life, he'd been determined to stay as far away as possible. After all, he was furious at her, wasn't he?

So why was it that he couldn't help but notice the intelligent gleam that shone in those tawny golden eyes, or the way that wide, full-lipped mouth of hers seemed to be made just to laugh? He'd never heard her laugh, Nick realized suddenly. Unexpectedly, it seemed like an omission that ought to be remedied.

"Then again," said Randy, frowning slightly, "I have to admit I wasn't expecting to find you here at all. If you don't mind my asking, just what exactly are you doing at Manero's Pizza Shack at six o'clock on a Friday evening?''

"Damned if I know," Nick muttered. He glared at his daughter across the table. She smiled back benignly.

"What was that?"

Turning in his chair to face her, Nick shrugged. "It was all Wendy's idea. She told me that team parents had to take turns providing transportation to and from the games. I found out yesterday that I'd been elected."

"Really?" Randy's frown deepened. "How odd."

At least that explained why none of the girls she'd contacted beforehand had needed a lift, she reflected. But what was this business about the team parents taking turns driving? She hadn't heard anything about that at all. Indeed in the past, it had always seemed as though there were more than enough cars around. Several of the girls on the team were already old enough to have their licenses, and most of those that didn't had boyfriends who were only too willing to play chauffeur. So why had Wendy seemed to think that her father's services would be necessary?

"What's odd?"

"That Wendy would have asked you to help out." Randy shook her head in confusion. Then a sudden thought struck her. "Unless maybe she thought she couldn't get you to come and watch her play any other way?"

"Don't be ridiculous," Nick snapped. "If Wendy had wanted me to come to the game, she would only have had to ask. I always take an interest in her activities, and she knows it."

"I'm not suggesting that you don't. I'm just trying to figure out why she would have thought your services were needed."

"Well," Nick said sheepishly, "to tell the truth..."

"Yes?" Randy prompted curiously.

"I wouldn't be at all surprised to discover that my daughter has been up to some game playing off the field as well as on."

"Game playing?" Randy's surprise was clearly evident in her tone. "What do you mean?"

Nick smiled. "Somehow I have a sneaking suspicion that more than coincidence was involved in getting the two of us together here tonight."

"You mean," Randy said incredulously, "that Wendy had something to do with it?"

Ruefully Nick nodded. "Right down to the seating arrangement, it looks like she thinks she's got us exactly where she wants us."

"But..." Randy sputtered. This just didn't make any sense at all! "Why on earth would she do something like that?"

"Well...er," Nick stammered uncomfortably. "I'm afraid this part gets a little hard to explain."

"Try me," Randy invited, leaning closer. Amid the noisy babble of teenage voices that surrounded them, it was difficult to hear what Nick was saying. But the way things were shaping up, she was determined not to miss a single word!

"Well you see she saw us talking the other day when I came to pick her up at soccer practice and somehow she seems to have gotten the idea that we were getting along pretty well..."

Randy's mouth gaped open comically.

"Her mother and I have been divorced for many years, and now that she's old enough to be developing an interest in the opposite sex herself, she's been encouraging me to find myself a nice, compatible woman and..."

"Yes?" Randy prompted, stifling an unseemly urge to laugh out loud. Why the poor man was actually blushing! For what was probably the first time in his entire life, he'd found himself in a position where he was not in full control, and now he couldn't figure out what to do.

After the hard time he'd given her before, she ought to be gloating over his predicament, Randy mused. So why was it that Nick's obvious discomfiture seemed to be having the opposite effect on her instead? Indeed, Randy realized with a start, witnessing this rare glimpse of vulnerability—this chink in what she'd assumed was an impenetrable suit of armor—made her feel more drawn to him than ever.

And that, Randy decided quickly, wouldn't do at all! It was bad enough she was so attracted to Nick Jarros when he was being deliberately antagonistic. She hated to think how she might react if he ever stopped! And there was only one way to ensure against that happening...

"Don't tell me," she said, baiting him deliberately, "that Wendy wants you to settle down and get married again?"

Nick glanced up, surprised by her tone. Damn, this woman was sure of herself!

"No, not quite," he drawled meaningfully, surprised to discover that he was enjoying their verbal sparring enormously. "In fact, just the opposite. I got the distinct impression she seemed to think a nice, torrid affair would be just the thing."

But if Nick was hoping that Randy would be shocked into silence, he found that he was in for a disappointment.

Instead, she threw back her head and roared with laughter. "And she chose *me* to be your partner?"

Well at least that settled one thing, Nick thought with a disgruntled frown. Now he knew what her laugh sounded like.

"I'm sorry," Randy sputtered, gasping for breath, "really I am." She looked up to realize they had drawn curious glances from all around the table. Quickly she lowered her voice. "It's just that the invitation was so unexpected, that's all."

"What invitation?" Nick frowned. "I told you this was Wendy's idea, not mine."

"Oh yes." Randy strove for composure. "Of course."

Nick glowered down at her. "I can see how upset you are by this whole thing," he said sarcastically. "If it will ease your mind at all, let me assure you that I am not in the habit of taking my daughter's suggestions."

"Never?" Randy tilted her head to stare up at him wide-eyed, savoring the victory she knew was at hand. My but it was nice getting some of her own back, for once.

"Never," Nick replied firmly.

"Oh." Smiling, she shrugged. "Well in this case, I have to tell you, you're making a big mistake."

She'd only been kidding, hadn't she? Randy asked herself two hours later. Quickly she answered her own question. Well of course she had. At the time, she'd wanted nothing more than to finally put the man in his place once and for all. So why hadn't that happened?

Because Nick had surprised her, Randy remembered. Instead of retaliating, he had risen to the occasion nobly, parrying her jest as though its obvious intimation didn't faze him at all. To top it off, that bold remark seemed to have finally broken through the ice between them. It was as though the act of acknowledging, even only tacitly, the attraction they felt for each other had freed them from the need to continue the defensive sparring that had characterized their other encounters.

To their mutual amazement, they'd both relaxed. As time went on, being the only two adults at the table, they'd gravitated toward another naturally. For once their differences had seemed unimportant; and when the talk around them centered on Boy George and the latest entertainment gossip, they'd turned to each other instead, finding a tentative common ground of shared interests.

The pizza had been delivered shortly and, disdaining the plastic knives and forks, Randy plopped a large stack of napkins beside her plate and ate with her fingers, licking them with lusty enjoyment after every bite. She watched out of the corner of her eye, noting that it wasn't long until Nick laid down his flimsy utensils and joined her.

During the meal, most of the talk centered around the game as the girls rehashed some of their successful plays. To Randy's surprise, she discovered that Nick had been an astute observer of the contest betweeen the two teams, and now the advice and commentary he offered about what he had seen was treated with respect. Deftly he fielded the girls' questions, sometimes answering them himself, and just as often referring them to Randy, who watched the easy rapport he built with the teenagers with growing admiration.

Somehow over the course of the meal, her chair seemed to have scraped its way back across the floor to its original position. Around the confines of the crowded table, Randy couldn't help but be aware of Nick's physical presence beside her as the conversation eddied around them. Seated shoulder to shoulder and thigh to thigh, her nose was teased by the light elusive smell of his aftershave. His body's warmth was a tangible presence, touching not only her skin but her senses as well.

The first two times their knees bumped beneath the table, Randy shifted away self-consciously. The third, she knew it had happened once too often to be purely accidental. Tilting her head up to his, Randy smiled inquiringly as she held her ground. Your move, she thought, waiting to see what would happen next.

She didn't have long to wait. Shifting ever so slightly in his chair, Nick continued his discourse on dribbling techniques while his hand dropped down ever so casually into his lap. Randy tensed in anticipation.

He was paying her back, she realized suddenly, getting some of his own back in kind for that outrageous remark she'd made earlier. Obviously, he was hoping for some sort of response. Well, Randy thought determinedly, she'd be damned if she'd give him the satisfaction—

Abruptly she froze as the tip of his forefinger made searing contact with her naked knee. Slowly he traced a gossamer light design that brought goose bumps rising to the surface of her flesh. Randy shivered slightly, thoroughly unnerved by his touch, as the finger drew slowly upward toward the hem of her shorts. Then, just when she was sure she could stand it no longer, all at once, the touch was gone. Slowly she expelled her breath in a long sigh.

"Well Randy, what do you think, is Mr. Jarros right or not?"

At the sound of her name, Randy jumped, turning to face Kate Burnett, her starting center forward, across the table. "Hmm?" she asked, hastily gathering her scattered wits back about her. "What did you say?"

"I said," Kate repeated, "do you think Mr. Jarros is right about the proper way to execute a penalty kick?"

Hrrmph, thought Randy, that didn't help her at all! How could she even begin to figure out whether he was right or not, when she hadn't even the slightest idea what he had said? Beside her, Nick cleared his throat softly. She turned her gaze to his and found that he was smiling down at her through eyes that glittered with barely suppressed amusement.

"Your move, coach," he murmured, his expression infuriatingly smug.

Scowling, Randy turned back to face the table once more. "Well," she said slowly, "he certainly has some interesting ideas, doesn't he?" Her knee nudged his under the table as she added with deliberate sweetness, "Then again, as to how well he might be able to carry them out, I'd say that remains to be seen.''

It was just as well that the waiter chose that particular moment to appear beside the table and start clearing away their plates, Randy decided. Glancing around the large room behind them, she realized that the party had already begun to break up. But it was also a shame it had to end so soon. For while the evening had lasted, she had enjoyed herself—and Nick's company—enormously.

"Let me walk you to your car," Nick offered.

Nodding, Randy climbed reluctantly to her feet. Was he really that anxious to get rid of her?

"I'll be right back," Nick said to Wendy as they walked away. "Why don't you gather up everybody who needs a ride while I'm gone?"

The parking lot seemed quiet after the noisy din of the pizza parlor, and Randy breathed in deeply of the warm, summer night air.

"What a relief," Nick sighed as the door slammed shut behind them. "I hope you don't feel that I was rushing you, but all at once I couldn't resist the temptation to get you off to myself for a few minutes."

"Oh?" Randy felt a warm glow that started at the top of her head, and worked its ways slowly down to her toes. "And why would you want to do that?"

"Guess," Nick said softly, his voice as heavy as the fragrant night air. He reached out to curve his arm around her waist. The gesture was warm and natural, without being intimate. It felt entirely right. Just as it felt right to Randy to lean into his hold, molding the length of her body into his.

It was amazing how in the space of two short hours, everything could have changed, Randy mused, realizing that as their antagonism had mellowed, a growing physical awareness had flowered in its place. The sparks that seemed to fly every time they came together were still very much in evidence. Now however, their source had changed, becoming something just as potent but infinitely more dangerous.

All too soon, they reached the spot in the middle of the lot where she'd left her car. As they stopped beside it, Nick drew her around to face him, his other hand reaching up to rest lightly on her shoulder.

"Thank you for seeing me to my car," said Randy, dismayed to hear the soft, husky quality of her voice.

"My pleasure." Nick's head bent low, his lips so near to hers that Randy could feel the moist warmth of his breath. "I'd really like to kiss you, Randy Wade," he murmured, as the arm that curled around her waist tightened slightly, pulling her closer still.

"I'd like that too." She sighed, knowing it was meant to be.

What was the use of fighting the inevitable, she thought, her eyelids flickering shut. All evening long Nick had held her in thrall. No man had ever had that effect on her before. Now, at last, she was going to find out why.

Then abruptly, even as she waited to savor his touch a shrill whistle rent the air around them. It was followed by a chorus of teenage voices, cheering rudely. "Yeah coach! Way to go!"

Immediately Nick jerked away, his hands dropping back quickly down to his sides. "What the hell...?" he growled angrily, his gaze sweeping around the lot.

Beside him, Randy shivered slightly, realizing that her lips were still pursed, her mouth still waiting breathlessly for the kiss that hadn't come.

Nick swore eloquently under his breath as he located the carful of teenage boys responsible. Reaching down, he jerked open the door to her car and slipped her inside. "I'll be damned if I'm going to provide a show for a bunch of underage Romeos!"

Damn! thought Randy, biting her lip in frustration. Talk about bad timing. She'd have given a year off her life for just one more uninterrupted moment in that parking lot with Nick. Then as she gazed upward at his thoroughly disgruntled expression, she realized that he was fighting an ache every bit as strong as her own. Unaccountably, that thought brought a tender smile.

"They're only kids," she said soothingly. "Don't be too hard on them."

Slamming the door to her car, Nick braced both hands on the sill of the open window and leaned down to look at her in the half-light. "Why the hell not?" he muttered fiercely, refusing to be placated.

Reaching up, Randy cradled his jaw lightly in the palm of her hand, tilting his face to hers. "At their age they're naturally curious," she said. "They're still trying to figure out all those things you've already known for years." Pausing, Randy shrugged. "If anything, you should be flattered, Nick. After all, they're smart enough to want to learn from the best."

Well I'll be damned, thought Nick, stepping back as she deftly maneuvered the car out of the space. He watched the twin set of receding taillights until they had crossed the lot and pulled out onto the street.

Then slowly he smiled. Someday he was going to get the last word with that woman, he vowed.

Four

Dear Aunt Miranda.

I don't mind telling you that I'm confused. As a teenage girl who has recently started to date, I have to admit I am having a hard time figuring the whole system out. My mother tells me that when a boy takes you out, he is supposed to pay your way. The girls at school say that that is the old-fashioned way—that now it's perfectly all right to "go dutch" as long as you're doing something you both want to do. To top it off, the boys seem to think that if they *do* pay for the entire date, then at the end of the night, you owe them something in return for all the money they have spent. (However my father, who was once a boy himself, says I should refer the next guy who tells me that to him, and he'll take care of it.)

Obviously you can see my dilemma. Everybody has a different opinion, and I have no idea who to listen to. All I want is to do the right thing. Can you help me straighten this out?

Signed,
Baffled By The
Whole Idea

Dear Baffled,

I hate to say this, but when it comes to dating, everyone's confused, even those of us who have been doing it for a while! Unfortunately, there simply is no right or wrong way to do things.

Your mother's correct in that, when she was growing up, the boy almost always did assume financial responsibility for the date. But thanks to the emergence of women's liberation, your friends are also right about how things are done today.

As for the next matter, I agree with your father. As far as I'm concerned, any boy who tries to tell you that you owe him something at the end of the night deserves little more than a swift kick (and you can feel free to place it wherever you think it will do the most good!) He's had the pleasure of your company all evening, and that is *all* his money entitles him to.

I know I haven't exactly answered your question but, believe it or not, I've done the best I could. If by any chance you do figure out how this curious institution called dating is supposed to work, please write back and let me know. I've often wondered that myself!

Signed,
Aunt Miranda

Nick called the following morning as Randy was sitting in her kitchen eating breakfast.

"I hope you don't mind that I'm asking on such short notice," he said, his voice flowing to her like warm honey through the telephone wire, "but I was wondering if by any chance you might be free for dinner tonight."

Randy hesitated, but only briefly. "Don't tell me, let me guess. Wendy's standing behind you right now, a shotgun aimed at your shoulder."

"Hardly," Nick drawled, chuckling softly. "In fact I'd have been tempted to call earlier, except that I couldn't find a good excuse to get her out of the house before this. Believe me, this is strictly my own idea. Wendy has nothing to do with it."

Randy smiled radiantly. "In that case, I'd love to," she enthused, and they quickly completed the arrangements.

It was interesting the way things sometimes worked out, Randy mused as she hung up the phone. Three days ago, she'd have been happy to strangle Nick Jarros with her bare hands. Now she was looking forward to their date with unconcealed delight.

In some ways, it didn't make any sense. In others, the implications were all too clear. Nick was a vital, attractive, and compelling man—a man who, for someone with her limited range of experience, was way out of her league. It would be easy, Randy reflected, for her to let herself get caught up in that alluring magnetism that was so much a part of his presence. Hadn't her response to him the previous night shown her that?

Looking back now at the way she'd behaved, Randy shook her head disparagingly. If she didn't know better, she'd have said she'd been flirting with Nick. Oh maybe not in the conventional sense. Certainly there'd been no fluttering eyelashes, no coyly averted gazes. Instead their byplay had taken the form of thrust and parry—a game of one upmanship that they'd both enjoyed with a vengeance.

Of course from what she'd seen, there wasn't anything conventional about Nick Jarros anyway, Randy mused. So why should she expect her response to be any different? But still, *flirting* for Pete's sake? That had to be a first!

And it was Nick who had been responsible for the change. Clearly the man was different from any she had ever known—a man who made his own rules and didn't give a damn what other people thought of them. He excited and infuriated her all at the same time. Taken together, the two were a potent combination. And, Randy thought with a heady thrill of anticipation, an irresistible challenge.

She stared out across her kitchen dreamily, seeing nothing but the image of a granite-carved face with cool, chinablue eyes. So she was finally learning to flirt, was she? Maybe it was about time.

That evening, Randy dressed for her date with care. So far, the three times Nick had seen her, she'd been dressed to suit the job at hand. Tonight, Randy reflected, there would be nothing practical at all about the outfit she chose.

Combing through her closet, she pulled out a peach and white striped silk in a deceptively simple shirtwaist style. It was a dress that looked like nothing on the hanger, and a million dollars when she had it on, relying as it did on a superb cut, lightly padded shoulders, and the marvelous drape of the fluid silk to mold itself to her figure in a way that was outrageously flattering.

Checking her reflection in the full-length mirror on the back of her closet door, Randy added a white patent leather belt, then bloused the soft material over it, adjusting the dress so that it would sway seductively around her slim hips when she walked. A pair of white strappy sandals with high spike heels added several inches to her tall slender frame, and Randy surveyed the results with satisfaction.

Randy was ready with five minutes to spare, which was lucky because Nick was early. He rapped sharply on the door twice, and she opened it immediately to find him standing on the step, holding in his hand a single, perfect red rose.

For a moment she was quite speechless, letting her gaze sweep over him, and taking in the details of his appearance from the impeccably tailored navy blazer, down the slim-fitting khaki pants, to the highly polished loafers he wore without socks. His oxford cloth shirt was pink, and the tie knotted over it was a narrow burgundy foulard, the perfect final touch.

Randy had thought him impressive in blue jeans, but that was nothing compared to the way he looked to her now. The aura of blatant masculinity was still present, but now it combined with something else—an air of power, she decided, of totally assured self-confidence, that emphasized his sexuality in a way that was immensely appealing.

"Well?" Nick asked with a mocking grin. "Do I pass muster?"

Abruptly, Randy came to, realizing with no small amount of embarrassment, that she had left him standing on the step. "You'll do," she retorted, opening the door wide to let him inside. She pushed it shut, then turned to find that he was assessing her as well, his gaze roaming down over her body with easy familiarity before the blue eyes returned to her face, and he nodded his approval.

"Very nice," Nick commented, smiling down at her. "I like your dress. Although in your case, it might be considered gilding the lily."

"Thank you." Randy smiled in return, more pleased by the compliment than she cared to admit. Talk about polish, she thought wonderingly. He might not always be inclined to show it, but when he did, the man certainly had style!

"Is that for me?" she asked, nodding toward the rose. "Or do you just happen to be carrying a flower around with you?"

"Tut, tut." Nick shook his head. "Grabby little thing, aren't you?"

Playfully Randy threw back her shoulders and drew herself up to her full height. "Who're you calling little?" she demanded, amazed to discover that, for the first time in her life, she felt, if not petite, at least not overwhelmingly tall, either.

"I stand corrected," Nick agreed with a grin, and Randy followed the line of his gaze downward to find his gaze centered on the provocative thrust of her breasts against the thin bodice of her dress.

It was clear that his comment had nothing whatsoever to do with her height, and Randy groaned inwardly. Oh no, what had she started now?

"You're not little at all," Nick added, his voice low and sensuous. "In fact, I'd say you were just right."

"Chauvinist," she muttered under her breath, wondering if he was one of those pseudoliberated men who felt obliged to leap to their own defense.

"Of the worst sort," Nick agreed easily, taking the wind from her sails. "Now are you going to find a vase for this rose, or am I going to be forced to hold it until it wilts in my hands?"

"Coming right up," said Randy, just as pleased by the change of topic. In the kitchen, she quickly located a cut-glass bud vase, filled it with water, then slipped the single bloom inside.

"Do we have time for a drink?" she asked, as she set the flower down on the marble ledge above the fireplace, "or would you rather we were on our way?"

Nick glanced down at the slim gold watch on his wrist. "If you don't mind, I think we'd better go. I've made reservations at an inn down in Ridgefield, and if we leave now, we should just about make it."

The drive south was a lovely half-hour interlude. As Nick piloted the Ferrari down the winding country roads, Randy leaned back in the plush leather bucket seats, enjoying the music that drifted from the stereo and the twilight view of the countryside that surrounded them. A strangely companionable silence seemed to fit both their moods, and Randy could only marvel at how comfortable she felt in the presence of a man who, for all intents and purposes, was still very much of a stranger.

Their destination turned out to be a quaint, white clapboard inn built in the eighteenth century, which housed a restaurant of thoroughly modern repute. They were seated in a small, quiet, dining room with a view overlooking a sparkling brook. Rather than handing out menus, the waiter simply recited the specialties from which they made their selections.

"This place is really lovely," Randy said, as the waiter returned with their predinner drinks. "How did you ever find it?"

"A client that I did some work for in Danbury recommended it. I've been coming here on special occasions ever since."

Randy's smile glowed softly in response to his words. What a lovely thing for him to say! It was a moment before she realized that she was staring at him dreamily across the linen covered table. Quickly, she pulled her gaze away.

Watch yourself Wade, she thought, lifting her scotch and soda and sipping at it determinedly. At this rate, she would be putty in his hands before they even reached the main course!

"Is that so," she commented, then quickly changed the subject. "You know, speaking of your work, I have been curious—ever since you stormed into my office in the middle of the day to be exact—about what it is that you do for a living."

"Is that so important?" Nick countered, watching her over the rim of his glass.

Randy shrugged. "In the sense that it would make any difference to me, no. In the sense that what you spend your days doing has a great deal of bearing on who you are, yes." She paused, then added with a smile. "I'm not trying to be nosy, it's just that I can't help but wonder. After all, there are few men whose jobs permit them to be available during the week, whenever their daughter needs them."

"Yes, you're right, there are," Nick agreed. "In that regard, I've been very lucky. As you may have guessed, I work freelance. I work at home, and I'm able to set my own hours."

"Very good." Randy nodded, her eyes dancing impishly. "But what exactly do you *do*?"

"Oh yes." Nick grinned in response. "I did forget to mention that part, didn't I? I design computer software."

Randy groaned softly. She should have known!

"Something the matter?" Nick asked, looking at her curiously.

"I hate to say this," Randy admitted, "but you're looking at a woman who's absolutely hopeless when it comes to machines. For years now, I've been hoping that computers will turn out to be no more than a passing fad."

"Really?" Nick choked back a laugh. "Don't tell me, let me guess. You were frightened by a runaway vacuum cleaner when you were a little girl, and you haven't been able to look a machine in the eye since."

"Nothing so dramatic, I'm afraid. It's just that anything mechanical has me baffled. I know I'm an intelligent person and I should be able to handle them. Yet for some reason, all I have to do is look at the word processing machines we have down at the paper, and I break out in a cold sweat."

"Maybe your problem is that you've never been properly introduced."

Randy looked up in surprise. "Introduced to a computer? You are kidding me, aren't you?"

"Not really," said Nick. "After all, everybody has to start somewhere."

"You may be right," Randy replied, not sounding entirely convinced. "All right, you're the expert around here. Tell me how you got started."

Nick shrugged. "The beginning was accidental. I married young and needed a job. At the time, a number of the large firms were actively seeking people to come and take part in their computer training programs. It turned out that I had an aptitude for problem solving. Pretty soon, whenever anyone needed a program that could fulfill a specific function, they came to me and I designed the software for them.

"After my wife and I got divorced, I had Wendy to think about. I didn't want to continue working in a job that was going to keep me away from my daughter for hours, or even days on end, so I quit and went out on my own."

"You must have been very good to be able to make a go of it," Randy commented as the waiter delivered their food, and they began to eat.

"I am," said Nick. "But remember, all this happened a dozen years ago, so I was also one of the first, and that helps. By the time the field became crowded, I had already built up enough of a reputation that I didn't have to worry about where my next job was coming from."

Randy nodded silently, wondering about something he had said as she cut into the thick, juicy slab of rare roast beef on her plate. Taking a large bite, she chewed slowly and carefully as she pondered how to broach the subject.

"Did I say something wrong?" Nick asked, and she looked up to find him gazing at her across the table. "Or are you just one of those people who don't like to talk and eat at the same time?"

"Neither," Randy said sheepishly. "Actually, it's more that I want to ask another question, and I can't quite figure out how to do it without sounding too pushy."

"Just ask away," Nick advised with a grin. "That's what I always do."

"Okay I will." Randy laughed. "But just remember, you're the one who asked for it." She paused, waiting for Nick's nod of assent before continuing. "A few minutes ago, you said that after you and your wife were divorced, you had Wendy's welfare to consider. I know times are changing, but isn't it still customary for the mother to be given custody in the case of a young child? I was just wondering how it happened that she came to live with you."

Abruptly Nick's grin faded. "It's really very simple," he replied. Suddenly there was a grim edge to his tone that made Randy rue the impulse that had made her ask the question in the first place. "Her mother didn't want her."

"Didn't want her?" she echoed, her face mirroring the shock that she felt. "How is that possible?"

"You don't know how many times I've asked myself exactly that same question," Nick said harshly. "June and I were only married for a little less than three years and, although it sounds strange, you might say I never got to know her well enough to really understand what made her do the things she did."

Gazing at him from across the table, Randy felt her heart go out to him, as her natural empathy asserted itself. What kind of woman could his wife have been to turn her back not only on her husband, but also on her own child?

"Don't look so sad," said Nick, interrupting her thoughts. "I guess maybe what they say about every cloud having a silver lining is true. At least in this case, it certainly was. I have Wendy, and I couldn't be happier with the arrangement."

Spearing a piece of meat, Randy lifted it slowly to her mouth. "Does her mother ever come to see her?"

Frowning, Nick shrugged. "Occasionally, but not very often. She lives in Washington, D.C., now working as a professional lobbyist. From what she tells me, she's a very busy lady. But then, she always was. I guess that's what came between us in the first place."

"How so?"

Nick paused for a moment, considering his answer before speaking. Over the years, he'd thought back on his failed relationship with June as little as possible. Certainly he'd never discussed it with anybody before. Yet somehow, with her gentle prodding and quiet support, Randy had a way of making him want to talk, to air the grievances that had marred both that early marriage, and the life he had built for himself since.

"June and I were both very young when we got married," he said slowly. "Too young, although of course we didn't think so at the time. It wasn't until it was too late that we discovered just how ill-suited we really were. I know it may seem old-fashioned to you, but the image of married life that I'd grown up with included a husband who was the breadwinner and, once there were children, a wife who was happy to stay at home and devote herself to the family."

"I take it your wife didn't agree?"

"That's putting it mildly," Nick snorted. "It didn't take June long to discover that she was bored running a household. She knew I didn't want her to work, especially since

Wendy was only an infant at the time, so instead she decided to become "involved."

"For weeks at a time, I never knew what she'd be into next. If she wasn't out protesting Nixon, then she was organizing the neighborhood blockwatch. She ran local campaigns to save first the seals, and then the whales. You name it, my wife was a part of it."

Nick held up a hand to stop Randy's automatic protest. "I know what you're thinking, and I agree. It's not that those aren't all worthy causes. But June became such a fanatic that she threw herself into them to the detriment of her family. Somehow she was always the one who was needed to work overtime, or the one who volunteered to drive two hundred miles to deliver pamphlets to a last-minute rally."

Shaking his head slowly, Nick shrugged. "The marriage simply couldn't stand up under that kind of neglect. In the end, the relationship simply withered away; she went her way and I went mine."

"I see," Randy said softly. Finishing her meal, she lined up her knife and fork on the edge of the plate.

Well at least that explained one thing. All at once, the extreme reaction he'd had to her column was beginning to make sense. After one bad experience with a woman who'd made it her life's work to become involved in everybody's business but her own, she could just imagine how he must have viewed Aunt Miranda—as yet another busybody who made her living by meddling in other people's lives. No wonder he'd been so upset!

"But enough about that," Nick said firmly as the waiter appeared to clear their plates. "As Wendy would probably be only too happy to tell you, it's been quite some time since I've had the pleasure of escorting a beautiful woman out on a date. As you may have noticed, I'm a little rusty." He paused, smiling sheepishly. "Otherwise I'm quite sure I never would have bored you with the maudlin tale of my first marriage.''

"Is that so?" Randy countered with a grin. "Well maybe it's a measure of how rusty I am myself, but to tell you the truth…" Her voice dropped to a low, confiding whisper, "I wasn't bored in the slightest."

"I'm glad," said Nick.

His smile was endearingly boyish, and with a start Randy realized just how susceptible she was to its appeal. As he'd talked, her heart had opened to him instinctively. Now, however, in this light teasing mood, he was even more attractive than ever.

"Can I get you anything else?"

Randy glanced up quickly as the black-suited waiter appeared beside them once again, this time to recite the rest of the menu before taking their order for coffee and dessert.

"Tell me the truth," said Nick when the two steaming cups of Irish Coffee they'd both decided on had been delivered. "Are you really as rusty at this as I am, or did you just say that to make me feel better?"

Randy chuckled. "Guilty as charged, I'm afraid."

Nick's dark eyebrows lifted incredulously. "How can that be? I can certainly see why a single parent like me might not be inclined to spend too much time painting the town red, but a lovely, unattached lady…?" His voice trailed away, letting the question hang in the air.

"Even we unattached singles have our responsibilities," Randy pointed out, sipping her hot coffee cautiously. "I may not have any children of my own, but sometimes, between my two jobs, I feel as though I've adopted the whole town."

Nick nodded, his blue eyes pensive. "If you don't mind my asking, just how did you end up as the coach of the girls' soccer team anyway?"

"It was a fluke, pure and simple. One of the girls wrote to Aunt Miranda in the spring, complaining that although the boys had intermural teams that played games during the summer, there were no comparable programs for the girls. She didn't think it was fair, and neither did I. We ran an editorial in the paper, drummed up some local support, and eventually the school board caved in to the pressure."

"That explains where the team came from," Nick pointed out, "but not how you ended up as coach."

Randy grinned ruefully. "Much as I'd like to say they chose me for my superior ability and sterling qualifications, the truth of the matter is, we couldn't get anybody else to volunteer. As I keep telling myself, I may not be the best coach the sport has ever seen, but I'm better than nothing."

"Quite a bit better," Nick said quietly, "if that first game the girls played was any indication."

He was trying to apologize for the things he'd said that day on the field, Randy realized, knowing that Nick was not the sort of man to whom such a gesture would come easily. Smiling, she shrugged modestly. "I hate to admit it, but the season opener was one of the easiest on our shedule. Of course I'm glad we won for the girls' sakes, but I wouldn't necessarily expect our success to continue."

"Oh I don't know," said Nick. "You cut quite a figure standing out there on the sidelines last night in that skimpy little outfit of yours. From the looks that guy who was coaching the other team kept giving you, I'd say he was lucky he remembered he had any players on the field at all."

"He...who...*what*?" Randy's mouth opened, then snapped shut. What on earth was he talking about? At yesterday's game, she'd been wearing a pair of perfectly respectable shorts and a tee shirt. Surely he wasn't accusing her of trying to purposely provide a distraction?

"You know what I mean," Nick replied with thoroughly infuriating calm. "With a figure like yours, I'm sure it's happened before."

So that was it, thought Randy, bristling defensively. In his own, roundabout way, Nick was letting her know that he'd noticed the size of her chest. She should have known it would happen eventually. It always had before.

"If you don't mind," she said primly, "I'd rather not discuss it."

Nick's eyebrows lifted in surprise. "You'd rather not discuss it? Is that any way to respond to a compliment?"

"A compliment?" Randy snorted in disbelief. "Is that what that was?"

"Of course. What else could it have been?"

Scowling, Randy muttered a few choice words under her breath. "Men! You're all alike!"

Frowning in reply, Nick set his coffee mug down on the table with a loud thump. "I resent that!"

"Good," Randy said sweetly. "I'm glad you know how it feels, because for years now, I've resented the fact that every time a man looks at me, his eyes head downward automatically to check out the merchandise."

"I should think you'd be flattered by the appreciation," said Nick. "After all, there aren't many women with assets like yours."

"Terrific." Randy groaned softly. Her eyes pierced his across the table. "Just how flattered would you be in my place, knowing that all that appreciation had nothing to do with you as a person, but centered instead on the realization of someone's juvenile mammary fixations—"

"Juvenile?" Nick repeated incredulously then, shaking his head, added, "*Mammary fixations?*"

But Randy was on a roll now, and she refused to be deterred. "Believe me," she said, "it's bad enough to have the guys in school call you Big Randy when you're tall; even worse when you realize that's not what they're referring to!''

Seated across from her, Nick tried valiantly to keep a straight face. That he wasn't succeeding became increasingly obvious as his lips, which refused to stop twitching, broke finally into a broad grin.

"It isn't funny!" Randy stormed.

"Lady," Nick cried, beginning to laugh out loud, "you don't know the half of it!"

Frowning, Randy could only sit and watch helplessly until at last he had gotten his amusement back under control. "Now," she said pointedly when his chuckles had finally subsided, "if you don't mind my asking, just what was that all about?"

Nick took a final, cleansing breath. Across the table, his eyes found hers and held them. "At this point, it would probably make more sense for you to ask what it was not about—"

"Oh for Pete's sake!" Randy snapped. "What was that supposed to mean?"

"What it was not about," Nick continued calmly, ignoring the interruption, "was the size of your breasts. In fact, to tell the truth until you mentioned it, I hadn't even particularly noticed." Pausing, his eyes skated downward briefly, then returned to her face. He shrugged with oddly disarming candor. "Can I help it if I'm a leg man?"

"Legs?" Randy repeated in dismay. He had to be kidding! she thought wildly. She'd seen her legs and there was nothing particularly notable about them. They held her up, and they reached the floor. As far as she was concerned, that was about all there was to them. "*Those* were the assets you were referring to?"

"'Fraid so," Nick said with a smile.

Randy had never been much of one for blushing, but now she could feel the heat staining her cheeks a vivid shade of pink. "You mean you weren't..."

Nick shook his head, his eyes twinkling. "I'll let you in on a little secret," he confided. "As these things go, I'm a purist. I make it a habit never to pass judgment on anything I haven't personally seen for myself."

Oh good lord, Randy gulped, feeling as though the flush that had warmed her face had now spread downward to radiate its heat throughout her entire body.

She couldn't think of anything at all to say to that so instead she simply remained silent. Nick too, seemed lost in thought as they quickly finished off their drinks, paid the check and made their way back out to the car.

On the ride down, Randy had been lulled by the beautiful scenery. Now the mood was set by the dark, starry sky that surrounded them, enveloping the small car in its seductive spell. Leaning back to rest her head on the seat, Randy was vibrantly aware of Nick's presence beside her. She watched the way his fine, long-boned fingers grasped the polished knob of the stick shift; saw the subtle play of muscle beneath the cloth of his pants as the car gathered speed and changed gears. He drove, she mused dreamily, the same way he did everything else—with the absolute assurance of a man who knew exactly what he was doing. By the time they'd reached her house, Randy had come to a decision. Wherever it might lead, she did not want her evening with Nick to end just yet.

"How about a nightcap?" she suggested, as they climbed from the car. Without waiting for his reply, she turned and headed for the front door.

Silently, Nick watched her walk away, her bearing regal as she traveled the moonlit path. Damn, but he was tempted! Once he walked through that door, she'd be his till morning, he just knew it. Never before had he been faced with a prospect that pleased him so much. But he simply couldn't allow himself to give in. It was too much, too fast. He'd made that mistake once before and spent the rest of his life paying for it. He was older and wiser now. This time around, things would be different. They had to be.

Swearing softly in frustration, he followed her up the path. By the time he reached her side, the door was already open and she had stepped inside to turn on the light. "Randy," he said softly, stopping on the porch.

Her eyes wide, she turned to look at him in the half-light.

"I'm afraid I can't come in."

"Oh?" Randy paused, biting her lip uncertainly. That was the last thing she had expected.

Slowly, Nick shook his head. "I have to be getting back. I have Wendy to think about after all..." Lamely his voice trailed away. Even to his own ears, the excuse sounded weak.

"Of course," Randy said quickly, covering her confusion with a smile that was overly bright. "I understand."

Lord, but she'd really done it now! she thought, cringing inwardly with embarrassment. How could she have been so wrong? She'd have sworn, especially after their parting last night that Nick was every bit as attracted to her as she was to him. Yet now, from the way he'd responded to her invitation, it was perfectly obvious that he couldn't wait to escape.

If that was the case, Randy thought spiritedly, she certainly wasn't going to detain him. Meeting his gaze coolly, she extended her hand to his. "Thank you very much for a lovely evening—"

"Oh hell!" said Nick.

His fingers closed roughly over hers, pulling her closer across the small space that separated them until Randy was supremely aware of the breadth of his shoulders beneath the tailored jacket; the musky, compelling scent of his body;

and the faint shadow of stubble that lined his jaw. Startled, her eyes sought his and found them riveted to her mouth. Her lips trembled, then parted beneath his gaze, and Randy drew a deep, uneven breath at the sudden burst of longing that sang through her veins.

She knew she ought to step back, withdraw her hand from his, maybe even make some teasing remark to lighten the mood. But her feet refused to carry her away, and when she opened her mouth, no sound came out at all. A moment later, when Nick slowly drew her to him, Randy knew that his kiss was inevitable and that he hadn't left because he wanted it every bit as much as she did, maybe even more.

With incredible tenderness, Nick's fingers flickered across her temple, then down the softness of her cheek until they cupped her chin lightly, raising her face to his as he pulled her forward into his arms. Her actions purely instinctive, Randy tilted her head back to his. Her eyelids slowly closed. She felt the warmth of Nick's breath mingling with her own before his lips came down to claim hers in a series of light, feathering kisses that asked everything and demanded nothing, tantalizing her senses with the teasing promise of pleasures to come.

He parted her lips with his tongue, gaining access to the softness within, and Randy surrendered herself fully to his embrace, feeling suddenly weightless, buoyed by a curious floating sensation, as though her body no longer existed at all, and the entire core of her being was centered around the warm hollows of her mouth when Nick's tongue lingered in sweet exploration.

What is happening to me, she wondered dazedly, savoring the kiss, even as she marveled at the potent magic of its effect. This tumultuous invasion bore no resemblance to the lovemaking she'd known before—the politely skilled caresses she'd accepted or deflected at will. No this kiss was something else entirely—an elemental life force driving far beyond the civilized boundaries she had yet explored—a sweeping, stirring, undeniable invitation to engage in the most primitive of interactions between a man and a woman. This kiss was a promise, and a beginning—daunting, yet at the same time, exhilarating to her senses in a way that Randy had never known before.

The tip of Nick's tongue traced a slow, sensuous path along the soft tissue of her inner lip, and she moaned deeply in response. Her purse fell, unheeded, to the floor at her feet. In the back of her mind, some small, remaining spark of rationality insisted that that was a terrible way to treat a fine piece of Italian leather, but at the moment, Randy couldn't have cared less, knowing only that now her hands were finally free to caress the strong, hard body before her.

Wrapping her arms around Nick's neck, she threaded her fingers through the soft ringlets of hair at his nape, then used this leverage to draw him closer still. Her own tongue darted forward to tease and torment in kind, her impulses taking free rein, as she was filled with a dawning sense of wonder at the glowing intensity of her response.

"No!" Nick rasped suddenly, drawing his head away with a small anguished groan. "God, I must be out of my mind!"

Slowly Randy opened her eyes. In her bemused and breathless state, it was a moment before she assimilated what he had said. Then, gazing up at him, she frowned. As endorsements went, it was not exactly promising. Shrugging off his hands, she stepped shakily away.

"Was it really that bad?" she queried sardonically. "Or have I simply neglected to recognize another one of your backhanded compliments?"

"Bad?" Nick echoed blankly. His eyes fell to her lips. They were red and swollen from his kiss, and he groaned softly at the shaft of desire that pierced suddenly through him. Angrily, he shook his head to clear it. He was thirty-six years old, for God's sake! Where was his control when he needed it most?

"I have to go," he said, making no attempt to move away.

"Yes, I know." Randy frowned. "Wendy, right?"

"Right." Nick nodded. As if the sound of his daughter's name had released him, he found he was finally able to move. Turning away, he hopped quickly down the three steps from the porch, and strode across the yard to the driveway.

Reaching his car, Nick paused. As if drawn by irresistible strings, he turned and saw her still standing where he had left her, her body silhouetted by the muted glow from the light in the front hall.

"I'll call you," he said, his voice deep and husky in the stillness of the night air. Then he climbed into his car and was gone.

I'll call you? Randy repeated to herself skeptically as she prepared for bed several minutes later. That had to be one of the oldest lines in the book. From her experience, it could mean anything from a promise to be in touch soon, to a polite, if insincere, brush-off. Which one, she wondered, did Nick have in mind?

With a deep, heartfelt sigh, Randy switched off the light and climbed in between the cool sheets. Moments later when she drifted off to sleep, there was a smile upon her face; the last thing she'd been aware of was the heady fragrance of a single deep-red rose.

Five

———

Dear Aunt Miranda,

Am I ever in a jam! Yesterday, while I was at school, my mother went snooping around in my room. She found my diary, and read the whole book, cover to cover! When I came home, she gave me the third degree about every single thing in there, and then grounded me for the rest of my life!

Aunt Miranda, you've got to tell her that she's being unreasonable. My diary may not be the tamest book around (but then, neither is the Bible!). Besides, half the stuff that's in there is more wishful thinking than fact anyway. I thought that's what a diary was supposed to be—a *private* record where a girl could feel free to say anything she wanted.

I know she's my mother, but don't teenagers have any rights at all? I say she had no business going through my things in the first place. She says she did what she did for my own good, but that she will abide by whatever you decide.

Signed,
Hoping for Justice

Dear Hoping,

I've got good news for you (and bad news for your mother). No matter what that diary of yours said, she had no right to read it. Everybody knows that a diary is one of the last bastions of privacy known to man. Whether she thinks she was looking out for your best interests or not, your mother was not playing fair by spying on you when you were not around to defend yourself.

The most important ingredient in any relationship (whether between a man and a woman, a mother and her daughter, or whatever) is trust, and you are justified in feeling that yours has been betrayed. When that goes, inevitably something very valuable is lost. You and your mother are both going to have to work hard to rebuild the faith you had in each other.

To begin with, your mother owes you an apology and a promise that she will never do such a thing again. For your part, depending on just how biblical those exploits of yours were, I'd be willing to bet you owe her a darn good explanation!

Signed,
Aunt Miranda

To Randy's surprise, Nick's phone call wasn't long in coming. He caught her the following morning as she sat hunched over the Sunday *New York Times* crossword puzzle, and proposed an afternoon's outing to a polo match down in Fairfield County.

"This time I confess, Wendy does have something to do with the invitation," Nick chuckled, his amusement reaching out to her through the wire. "It seems that one of the players on the Ox Ridge Team is simply *too much*—" his voice broke in an imitation of a teenage falsetto "—so it was her idea in the first place, although it did occur to me that someone who likes sports as much as you do might enjoy the game as well."

"I'd love to come," Randy enthused. "But I've never been to a polo match before. I hope you won't mind having to explain what's going on."

"Don't worry," Nick assured her. "Wendy and I have been to dozens. You know how girls are about horses. We'll be happy to show you around."

The afternoon was bright and clear and seasonably hot, and Randy dressed casually for the occasion in a brightly patterned sundress, whose camisole bodice was held in place by thin straps that tied on top of her shoulders. In deference to the heat, she wore only a minimum of makeup—a layer of brown mascara on her light, gold-tipped lashes, and a slick of peach-colored gloss on her lips. With any luck, she thought, after several hours of sitting in the sun, mother nature would supply the rest.

Once again, Nick arrived right on time. Today he was driving the jeep, and Wendy, who was bubbling with excitement about the upcoming game, climbed around into the back seat, relinquishing the place of honor beside her father to Randy. Then, leaning up to brace her arms on the backrest, the teenager kept them entertained throughout the ride with a running commentary on which of the players to watch.

"How did you two ever learn so much about the game?" Randy asked curiously, as Nick parked the jeep beside the field, then spread a blanket on the hood, forming a high perch from which they could sit and watch the action.

Wendy giggled. "It's really all my fault. When I was little, I was a real horse nut. I thought they were about the only thing that mattered in the whole world!"

"Sounds like the way you feel about boys now," Nick commented drily. He boosted both Randy and his daughter up onto the side hood, then climbed up to settle down between them.

"Oh daddy!" Wendy frowned. "Horses were just a passing phase, while boys are...well, you know!"

"I know enough to be hoping that this phase will pass too," Nick muttered under his breath, to Randy's amusement and his daughter's chagrin.

"Don't worry," Randy whispered, reaching across his lap to give Wendy's arm a reassuring pat. "I understand what you mean."

Wendy shot her a grateful glance, then turned all her attention to the field, as the two teams trotted out across the turf for the start of the game. "Oh look!" she squealed, waving excitedly at one of the players. "There's Reed now!"

Shading her eyes with her hand, Randy watched as the eight riders gathered into a tight bunch for the opening bowl-in that would start the game. "Which one is he?" she asked. As far as she could tell, in their matching uniforms with their heads covered by protective helmets, all the players looked alike.

"Over there." Wendy pointed downfield. A strong shot had sent the wooden ball flying toward the home team's goal, and the players thundered down the field after it. "The one riding the bay with the stockings."

"The bay?" Randy repeated, turning to Nick quizzically. "With stockings?"

He grinned at her baffled look. "Don't worry," he said, "you'll get the hang of it soon."

Under Nick's patient tutelage, Randy discovered a bay was a horse of reddish-brown color, while stockings were white markings on the legs that extended all the way up to the knees. Once she was able to sort out the different horses, he went to work on the riders themselves, explaining which ones played offense and which ones played defense then pointing out the significance of the various shots. By the end of the first chukker, Randy felt as though she had a pretty good idea of how the game was played.

She also had a pretty good idea that Nick approved of her dress, not to mention what was inside it. More than once, she had felt the steady heat of his gaze upon her and a surreptitious glance in his direction had confirmed her suspicions. Rather than following the game, his eyes were roaming slowly over her body, tracing the curve of her naked shoulders, or the long, slim line of her thigh.

He wanted to touch her, Randy realized. As the moments passed she felt his need as a palpable presence, shimmering in the moist, heavy air between them. And she wanted to touch him too—to feel once more the exquisite sensations she had experienced only hours before in his arms. If only it weren't for Wendy....

"So what do you think?" Nick's daughter asked. Her eyes were following the players dreamily as they trotted to the sidelines to change mounts, and Randy realized with a start that the chukker was already over. "Is Reed awesome, or what?"

Turning, Randy picked out the broad-shouldered player wearing a bright green jersey with the number three emblazoned across his back. Anything, she thought desperately. She'd use anything to take her mind off the man who was sitting between them in silence, his body as tightly tensed as a coiled spring.

"You're right," she agreed. "I'd say he's pretty awesome all right."

Beside her, Nick groaned loudly. "For God's sake, don't encourage her. That's all we need!"

Prompted by some inner devil, Randy let her gaze roam over the rest of the players. "If you ask me," she said, leaning across Nick's lap to confide to Wendy in a low, conspiratorial tone, "he's not anywhere near as awesome as number one over there." She gestured toward a well-muscled blonde who was exchanging his chestnut pony for a gray. "Now that's what I call a hunk!"

"I don't recall anybody asking you," Nick growled irritably, looking from one to the other. Women! One at a time was bad enough. Flanked by these two, he was definitely feeling outnumbered.

Both women blithely ignored him.

"Do you really think so?" Wendy trilled. She gave the blonde a long, appraising look. "Well I guess he's not bad, if you like that type. But for my taste, I'd say there are entirely too many muscles. He's probably all brawn and no brains, you know what I mean?"

Randy laughed appreciatively, while Nick continued to glare at them both in stony silence. "You may be right," she conceded. Straightening, she let her tawny-eyed gaze roam slowly up and down Nick's well-toned physique, before adding lightly, "It does seem that sometimes those muscle-bound types tend to jump in and lead with their left, before they really have any idea what's going on—"

"If you don't mind," Nick broke in, as the ponies trotted back out onto the field. "The second chukker is about to begin. I brought you here to watch the game, remember, not the boys that are playing it."

"Of course daddy," Wendy said meekly.

"That's goes for you too," he growled, frowning in Randy's direction.

"Of course, daddy," Randy echoed sweetly. She and Wendy exchanged a glance, then broke up in a flurry of delighted giggles, totally destroying the effect.

Good grief, thought Nick, his brow lowering in a scowl. As if it wasn't bad enough that he had to sit here beside her, pretending to watch the game and composing himself like some sort of statue; when in truth all he could think about was the sweet lemon scent of her hair, the way it shimmered in the afternoon sun, the way it fanned out like a red-gold cloud, curling downward over her breasts— Damn! Nick glowered at Randy irritably, then forced his eyes away. How dare she be checking out the local talent? And not only that, but comparing notes with his daughter about which ones she did or didn't find attractive. Didn't she even care that she was driving him mad?

At the end of the third chukker the spectators spilled out onto the field to trample the divots back down into the soft turf, while the ponies and the players took a much-needed break from the fast-paced game. Grasping Randy's hand in his, Nick led her purposefully off in another direction from the one his daughter had taken.

"Nick, what are you doing?" Randy cried, finding herself being dragged toward the far end of the field. "The divots we're supposed to be walking down are the other way."

"Hang the divots!" Nick roared, giving full vent to his frustration. He'd spent the last half hour watching her watch the players, wondering as her head turned this way and that to follow the play of the ball, which of the riders she had her eye on now. "We're going over there."

"So I see," Randy gasped, stumbling along behind.

"I want to talk to you!"

"So talk," Randy shot back, snatching her hand from his and stopping where she stood. "You don't have to drag me to New Jersey to do it."

Stopping as well, Nick spun to face her. "Since you don't understand the finer points of the game, I'm willing to give you the benefit of the doubt. But I think you should know that bleached-blond pretty boy of yours can't play worth a damn!"

"Bleached-blond pretty boy?" Randy echoed incredulously, starting to laugh. Was it possible, she wondered. Why he actually sounded jealous! "*Of mine?* Nick, what are you talking about?"

"And not only that, but in case you haven't noticed, he's way too young for you—"

"Of course he is," Randy agreed, controlling her merriment with effort. "From what I could see they all are."

Nick frowned in disbelief. "Then, if you don't mind my asking, why the hell have you been joining my daughter in ogling them all afternoon?"

"Oh for Pete's sake," Randy muttered, shaking her head. She reached out and took Nick's hand in hers. "Come on, hotshot. Let's walk, and I'll try to explain it to you."

"Well?" Nick prompted impatiently, when they'd gone several yards in silence.

"It's really very simple," said Randy. "If you'd ever been a girl, you'd understand perfectly—"

"If I'd been a girl," Nick countered quickly, his mood lightening as he favored her with a grin, "we wouldn't be having this conversation at all."

"Probably not," Randy agreed, matching his smile with one of her own. "But try to put yourself in your daughter's shoes anyway. At her age, fantasies are very important, and those boys she's watching play polo are the very stuff of which daydreams are made. Just the other day, I got a letter from a girl who was upset because her mother had read her diary. She was the first to admit that most of what she'd written was fiction, not fact."

Turning, Randy looked up in Nick's eyes. "Don't you see, especially for a girl like Wendy who isn't allowed to date, those fantasies of what life would be like if only she were, play a vital role. With the restrictions you've imposed upon her, she's testing her wings in the only way she can."

"All of which is another way of telling me, not too subtly, that you still think I'm being too strict with her."

Randy shrugged. "If the shoe fits..."

Reaching down, Nick cupped her chin in his palm, his long fingers cradling her jaw as he tilted her face up to his. "You know I'm only trying to do what's best for Wendy, don't you?"

Silently, Randy nodded.

"The trouble is," Nick continued, "that despite the first impression I had of you as a marauding do-gooder, I get the feeling that, deep down inside, you only want what's best for her too."

"I do," Randy confirmed softly. Her heart warmed as she realized what the admission had cost him. "I'm not asking you to push her out on her own, Nick, just to loosen the bonds a little—let her take a few chances, make few a mistakes...."

"But that's just it," said Nick. "When I was her age, I made plenty of mistakes, and I paid the price. I learned things the hard way. I don't want her to have to go through that."

"Nick, listen to me," Randy said seriously. "Sometimes finding things out the hard way is the only way. It's part of the learning process. It's also part of the process of growing up. No matter how much you might want to, you can't live your daughter's life for her."

For a brief moment, Nick contemplated her words in silence. Then unexpectedly, he smiled, the tiny lines that fanned out from the corners of his eyes crinkling with amusement.

"What's so funny?" Randy frowned, surprised by his sudden change of mood.

"You are," Nick replied, the smile widening into a full fledged grin. "Why is it, all of a sudden, I feel as though Randy Wade is gone, and instead I find myself stuck on a date with Aunt Miranda."

Randy frowned in reluctant admiration. He was good all right, she thought, realizing how deftly he'd managed to manipulate the conversation, turning the topic of discussion back to her without having made any concessions at all. Oh well. Randy shrugged resignedly. At least she'd tried.

"So you're feeling stuck, are you?" she challenged lightly. "Well we'll just have to see about that." Deliberately she turned away, avidly scanning the sidelines where the players were mounting their ponies, preparing to begin the second half. "You know," she mused aloud, "I've always had a thing about younger men, especially blondes..."

"Have you now?" Nick chuckled, not fooled in the slightest. The short, sharp blast of a horn signaled that play was about to begin, and they made their way back toward the jeep. "Well it's a good thing."

"What on earth do you mean by that?"

Nick shrugged disarmingly. "Well, I was afraid I was beginning to find I had rather a thing for a certain tall redhead, but now that I find I'm not your type, well—" he paused, his eyes alight with a devilish gleam "—I guess I don't have anything to worry about, do I?"

Mouth agape and quite speechless, Randy could only stand and stare as he strode away across the field.

There was, Nick reflected with a small private smile, a great deal of satisfaction to be gained from finally having the last word.

As the game progressed, Nick found his irritation returning. It took him the rest of the afternoon and a good part of
the evening to figure out why, and when he did, even he
himself was surprised.

He was jealous. It was as simple as that. Oh not of those
dashing, exuberant young polo players, he assured himself
quickly. Although he had felt a momentary twinge or two,
especially when he'd realized that for all Randy's denials,
they were probably closer in age to her than he was.

But no, that wasn't the real problem. Competition of that
sort he could handle, while this other thing had him totally
baffled. He was jealous of Randy herself—of the easy rapport she seemed to have built so effortlessly with his
daughter.

The two of them had spent the rest of the afternoon
chatting amiably about a variety of subjects, things that he
had never even known Wendy cared about, much less was
informed enough to discuss. Though it was obvious they
had tried to include him in their conversation, Nick had felt
like an outsider—an intruder who had somehow stumbled
into an alien land he did not understand at all.

Over dinner, a quick meal of hamburgers and fries that
they'd stopped and grabbed on the way home, their rapport had continued. To Nick's surprise, he had realized how
much he was able to learn about his daughter just by listening. Areas of her life where she'd automatically denied him
access, were apparently fair game when she had another
woman to confide in.

It was, Nick realized, as though Wendy, having been denied a woman's input for so long, now could not get
enough. And much as he hated to admit it, that thought left
him feeling seriously miffed. It wasn't easy being a single
parent, but dammit, he'd done his best!

For the last dozen years, he'd been the single most important thing in his daughter's life—a stable rock, a guid-

ing influence she knew she could always count on in times of need. So why suddenly did he feel as though the course of a single afternoon had changed all that? As though his place was being usurped by someone whose interference, no matter how well meaning, he found he couldn't help but resent?

Nor, Nick realized, did it help matters any that Wendy was feeling so insufferably smug about the way things had turned out. Bounding in the back door of the house that evening after they had dropped Randy off at her home, she had gone straight to the refrigerator, where she'd pulled out the milk and the chocolate syrup. Immediately Nick had known what was coming. Ever since she was a little girl, whenever he had wanted to have a heart to heart talk with her, he had started by fixing them each a steaming mug of hot chocolate.

Seated at the booth in the corner of the modern kitchen, Nick found himself smiling as his daughter fussed importantly over the ingredients on the stove. She really was growing up, he realized suddenly, seeing her in the role he himself had assumed for so many years. Every day she was becoming more of a woman and less and less a little girl. So why couldn't he seem to let go?

"Boy, what a day!" Wendy grinned happily as she delivered Nick his mug of hot chocolate, then slid in across from him in the booth. "Was that great, or what? That Randy is really something else, isn't she?"

"She certainly is," Nick agreed. Unaccountably, that niggling feeling of resentment that had simmered in his subconscious all day, rose once again to the fore. Determinedly, he pushed it back down, adding magnanimously, "Once you get to know her, she's really a very nice person."

"Nice?" Wendy cried, groaning theatrically. "Give me a break! She's stellar!"

Nick sipped at his hot chocolate in silence, refusing to follow her less-than-subtle lead. He'd be damned if he was going to fall into that trap. The last thing he needed was a daughter who felt it her right to comment on his social life.

"So," Wendy said casually, "when are you going to be seeing her again?"

Equally casual, Nick shrugged. "You heard for yourself that we didn't make any plans," he commented, then saw the slight flush that rose over Wendy's cheeks and knew the barb had hit home. Nick frowned, irritated with himself. Granted he had had a rough day, but baiting his own daughter? Was that any way for a grown man to behave?

Then again, he mused, it wasn't as though she didn't deserve the rebuke. Indeed, when he'd dropped Randy off at her door earlier, the only thing standing between him and the kiss he'd longed to take had been the avid interest with which Wendy had watched the entire proceedings from the car.

Didn't kids these days believe in giving their parents any privacy, Nick wondered irritably. Lord, how he'd ached to slip his arms around Randy and draw her close! But in the end, common sense had won out. Like it or not, he had to set a good example. Thinking back to the way Randy had turned her face up to his invitingly, her tawny eyes warm with a need that equaled his own, Nick shifted uncomfortably in his seat.

"Maybe not right then," said Wendy, "but that doesn't mean you couldn't call her and set something up."

Nick frowned crossly. Why were they having this conversation now, of all times? Couldn't she see he was in no mood to be pushed?

"You know," Wendy continued artlessly, "next week is the Fourth of July. Maybe Randy would like to come with us to see the fireworks—"

"Wendy, leave it alone all right!" Nick growled. After the day he'd had today, the last thing he needed was the prospect of another date with his daughter in tow.

"Sure," Wendy said softly, her voice clearly displaying the hurt she felt inside. "Anything you say. I was only trying to help...."

Seeing the look on her face. Nick immediately felt contrite. So the day hadn't turned out quite the way he had planned. That certainly wasn't Wendy's fault. "Hey, I'm sorry," he said, reaching across the table to enfold her hand in his. "I didn't mean to snap."

"That's okay." Wendy's deliberately careless shrug clearly indicated that it was anything but. "You don't have to see her again if you don't want to. It's just that *I* like Randy a lot. She doesn't talk down to me. And when I talk, she really listens."

"Of course she does," Nick replied gruffly, fighting a fresh stab of resentment without any success. He was hurting, and now his temper rose to assuage that pain. "She should. After all, that *is* Aunt Miranda's function in life, isn't it?"

Abruptly, Nick stopped, realizing what he had said. Now how had that slipped out?

"Aunt Miranda?" Wendy cried. She glanced up, looking suitably shocked. "What are you talking about?"

"Nothing," Nick said quickly. "Nothing at all." Lord, what had he gotten himself into now?

"What do you mean nothing?" Wendy persisted. "You can't just call Randy, Aunt Miranda, and then pass it off as nothing!" A smile spread slowly across her face as, with teenage glee, she sensed the presence of a secret about to be revealed. When she spoke, her tone was one of awe. "Is that really who she is?"

"Oh for Pete's sake." Nick scowled. "You don't have to talk about it as if it's the second coming. Everybody has a job, you know. It's not that big a deal."

"But Aunt Miranda!" Wendy breathed. "Wow! Wait until I tell the kids!"

"No!" Nick roared, then immediately paused. Good Lord, when had things gotten so out of hand? "You can't tell the kids," he continued in a more moderate tone. "You can't tell anyone. Randy doesn't want anyone to know."

"Oh," Wendy stuck out her lower lip in a disappointed pout. What good was a bit of juicy gossip if she couldn't pass it on? "Nobody at all?"

Firmly, Nick shook his head. "It's a secret."

"Okay." Wendy shrugged, and Nick was too relieved by her easy acquiescence to notice the way she crossed the two fingers that held the handle of her mug. "If that's the way you want it."

"It is," said Nick, relaxing back in his seat. That was close!

"Well I guess I'll be heading up to my room," said Wendy. Standing up, she crossed the room and rinsed out her mug in the sink.

"Isn't it a little early for bed?" asked Nick, glancing down at his watch.

Wendy shrugged. "Oh, I'm not going to bed just yet. Actually I thought I'd call a few girls on the team." She smiled disarmingly. "You know, girl talk?"

Nick regarded his daughter fondly. "I get the picture. Just don't stay on too long, okay? Remember, you have school tomorrow."

"Oh, daddy." Wendy leaned down quickly to plant a quick kiss on her father's cheek. "You worry too much, you know that?"

Watching as she strode from the room, her walk falling somewhere between a childish saunter, and a woman's provocative strut, Nick sighed deeply. Worried too much? he thought, shaking his head. The way things were shaping up, how could he help it?

The phone was ringing as Randy let herself in the front door of her house the following evening after work. She dashed through the living room, throwing down her purse and her keys on the couch, before grabbing up the receiver on the wall phone in the kitchen.

"Hello," she gasped, leaning against the wall and inhaling several deep gulps of air.

Maybe it was Nick, she thought hopefully, wondering if she should apologize for the well-meant, but obviously unwanted advice she'd directed his way. He'd seemed so preoccupied yesterday during the second half of the game that she'd begun to wonder. Later when he'd dropped her off, she'd hoped there'd be a chance to talk, but with Wendy sitting waiting for him the car, that had proved impossible.

Under Wendy's watchful gaze, he hadn't even had the nerve to kiss her, Randy realized, smiling at the memory. Indeed, he'd even seemed somewhat embarrassed by the fleeting peck she'd risen to her toes and brushed across his lips. Maybe he was calling to ask her out again, she thought. And this time, with any luck, they'd leave their chaperone at home.

All at once Randy frowned, realizing that the silence on the line had stretched to nearly a minute. "Hello?" she repeated questioningly. "Is anybody there?"

To her surprise, she heard only a brief flurry of high-pitched giggles before the connection was abruptly broken. Shaking her head, Randy placed the receiver back in its cradle. Oh well, she thought, one thing was sure, it hadn't been Nick. Probably just some kids playing a practical joke.

Turning away, she picked up her purse then went into the kitchen and began to prepare her dinner. She didn't give the incident another thought until several hours later when the second phone call came.

"Hello?" she tried again.

"Hi," said a deep male voice, whose tenor sounded suspiciously forced.

Once more, Randy found herself waiting through a long pause. "Is there something I can do for you?" she asked finally, making no attempt to hide her impatience.

"Er, I'm not sure." The voice cracked, then broke, emerging several octaves higher. "Is this really Aunt Miranda?"

Randy gasped as the implication of his words hit her. "Who wants to know?" she demanded, striving to recover her poise.

"That's not important," said the disembodied voice. He'd now given up on all pretense of a disguise, and Randy realized that her caller had to be no more than thirteen, or maybe fourteen, at the most. "I have this problem," he continued, "and I need to know what to do about it."

"I'm sorry," Randy replied quickly but firmly. "But I'm afraid I can't help you. Aunt Miranda only answers letters in the mail. If you'd care to send your question to her, care of the paper, I'm sure she'll be happy to answer it for you."

Randy frowned as the line clicked dead in her ear. Who was the boy, she wondered, and how had he known where to call? Everyone at the paper knew how important it was to guard her secret. She was sure one of them wouldn't have let it slip.

Yet, there was no mistaking the mysterious caller's message. Is this really Aunt Miranda? he had asked. He may have been hesitant about revealing his message, but as to her identity, he seemed very well informed. Too well informed, Randy mused.

What in the world was going on?

Six

Dear Aunt Miranda,

For a supposedly old lady, you sure are one good-looking fox. In fact, I've found myself developing a newfound interest in soccer that I had never before even suspected. That little uniform you wear to run around the field is *too* much! My only complaint is that you take that long, glorious, red hair of yours and tie it back in a braid.

Come on. Aunt Miranda, and give the guys on the sidelines a thrill. Wear it down just once and we'll be yours for life. (If you're looking for volunteers to help with the unpinning. I'm your man. I've had plenty of experience. If you know what I mean. Heh! Heh!)

I know you're pretty good at answering questions, so here's mine. Hey baby, are you busy Saturday night?

Just sign me,
The Stud

Shaking her head, Randy crumpled the letter into a small ball and tossed it overhand into her wastebasket. Surveying the mass of similar correspondence on her desk, she sighed deeply. It had been like this all week—first the phone calls, and now the letters.

First thing Monday morning, she'd questioned the rest of the staff, but everyone she'd spoken to had denied having any knowledge about the strange phone call she had received the night before. Hoping against hope that it had only been a fluke, she'd just about decided to ignore the whole thing when it had happened again. And then again. Indeed from the time she'd arrived home that night, until she left for work the following morning, it seemed as though her phone had never stopped ringing.

Not that it really helped matters any, Randy mused, but the majority of the callers had been sincere in their need to get in touch. Somehow in the minds of the ever-impatient teenagers, her function as Aunt Miranda had suddenly shifted from a write-in service to an instant phone-in hotline, where they hoped to have their questions answered on the spot.

Monday night she'd followed the same course of action she'd used with the first caller and referred them to the column. By Tuesday, out of sheer frustration, she'd begun to dole out small bits of advice. To her dismay, however, that only made matters worse. By Wednesday night, things had gotten so bad that she succumbed to the temptation and simply left her phone off the hook.

Then, as if that wasn't bad enough, this morning the letters had begun to arrive. Her normally full mail bag had been filled to overflowing with everything from thinly veiled propositions to invitations to next year's senior prom. Randy groaned aloud at the thought. If this continued much longer, she was going to go out of her mind!

"Hey kid, what's the matter?" Jenna Parks looked up from the next desk. "I can hear you gnashing your teeth from all the way over here."

Randy gestured toward the flood of letters on her desk. "You would be, too, if you had this mess to sort through."

"I should think you'd be glad to have so much mail. After all, isn't the purpose of the column to draw letters for you to answer?"

"Not letters like these," Randy replied grimly. Picking up one of the juicier examples from the top of the stack, she creased it into the shape of an airplane and sent it sailing across the aisle onto Jenna's desk. "Here, see for yourself."

Frowning, Jenna unfolded the note and began to read. Slowly her frown deepened. "Oh," she said, looking up sympathetically when she had finished. "I'm beginning to get the picture."

"Do you want to know the worst part?" Randy smiled ruefully. "I'm dying to blow my stack at somebody, but I can't figure out who. Somebody out there has made my life miserable, and I haven't the slightest idea who to blame."

Her head turning from side to side, Jenna surveyed the small office speculatively. "It really could have been almost anybody here," she pointed out, with a small shrug. "Just one small slip of the tongue..."

"I know." Randy gave a fatalistic sigh. "I suppose I'll probably never have the satisfaction of ambushing my tormentor in a dark alley—"

"Or it might even have been someone who isn't connected with the paper at all, like that hunk you told me about, whose daughter plays on the soccer team."

"Nick?" Randy glanced up quickly, her surprise evident. For some reason, the thought had never even occurred to her.

"Why not?" said Jenna. "He makes about as likely a suspect as anyone else."

"But he knew how imporant it was to me that nobody find out who Aunt Miranda was," Randy argued, having no idea why she felt compelled to leap so quickly to his defense.

Blithely Jenna shrugged. "Like I said before, it could have been an accident. Just one small—"

"I know," Randy finished for her, the wheels turning furiously in her brain. "Just one small slip of the tongue."

The more she considered the idea, the more likely it seemed. After all, everyone at the paper had already denied their involvement. And he was the one person she knew who had a direct line to the town's teenagers in the form of his daughter, Wendy.

Not only that, Randy mused, but after their date last Sunday, she'd been sure she'd hear from him again. On that score, however, there'd been only silence. Not that, with the way things were going, he'd have had an easy time getting through, but still...No, Nick was definitely lying low. Like a man who needed some time to think. Or, she reflected, like a man with a guilty conscience!

Randy glared down furiously at the pile of correspondence on her desk, First things first, she decided. For now, she would concentrate on getting this mess sorted and accounted for. But when that was done, she was going to confront Nick and find out just what exactly was going on.

Leaning down to reach around the side of her desk, Randy's fingers closed over the letter she had wadded up and tossed away. Defiantly she spread the crumpled paper back out on her blotter, skimming through it once more. Clearly, she thought, the only way out of this mess was to fight fire with fire.

Dear Stud,

   I am printing your letter only to serve as an example of what sort of correspondence I will not dignify with a reply in the future. This column is intended to be a service for people who are genuinely in need of help, not a clearinghouse for macho male fantasies. Bearing that in mind, I would appreciate it if you would kindly do your strutting elsewhere. (If you're as good as you say you are, I'm sure there are plenty of girls who would be willing to accommodate you.)

In answer to your question, as far as you are concerned, I am washing my "long, glorious, red hair" this Saturday night, and every other Saturday night of your natural life!

Signed,
Aunt Miranda

One of the advantages of living in a small town, Randy discovered that evening as she left work, was that everybody knew where everything was. A quick stop in the subscription department provided her with Nick's address, and one of the clerks there was only too happy to give detailed directions to the road in question. Fifteen minutes later, she had turned in at the mailbox labelled "Jarros" and was navigating a winding, rutted, dirt driveway that led off into the woods.

It was a good five minutes more before she reached the end, leaving the trees behind to come suddenly upon a majestic A-frame contemporary house that sat at the edge of a gently rolling meadow. It wasn't until then, as she drove up and parked beside the detached garage, that Randy began to experience her first moments of doubt.

What if Nick wasn't the one who had given her secret away, she wondered, climbing the steps that led to the front door. What if his silence over the past few days had been due to a lack of desire on his part, and not any guilty feelings she might have falsely attributed to him?

Frowning, Randy lifted the brass knocker and dropped it with a loud thud. Still, her misgivings refused to be silenced. What if he wasn't pleased to see her again? Indeed, what if he wasn't even home...?

At that moment, the door swung inward, answering at least one question in the affirmative. Nick Jarros was definitely home. It was also immediately apparent that she should have called before stopping by, Randy realized, taking in the details of Nick's appearance in a glance. Obviously she had come at a bad time.

It was clear that he wasn't expecting company for he was dressed, if you could call it that, in nothing more than a pair of torn, faded, cut-off blue jeans, that rode low on his hips and high on thighs, and gave new meaning to the phrase "dressed to kill."

She ought to know, thought Randy, feeling suddenly as though someone had delivered a lethal blow to her solar plexus. Slowly her eyes skimmed up and down, missing nothing from the casually mussed appearance of his dark hair, to the questioning gaze in his clear blue eyes, to the thick pelt of reddish brown curls that covered the well-defined muscles of his chest.

All at once, Randy felt an irrational urge to reach out and brace her palms against his naked chest. She wanted to feel the warmth of his skin and the beating of his heart beneath her hands. She gritted her teeth in silent frustration. Why did she have to be so angry at somebody who looked like that?

"Hi," she managed weakly, covering the low breathy quality of her voice with what she hoped was a bright smile. "I hope I haven't come at a bad time?"

"Daddy, who is it?" Wendy bounded down the stairs from the upper loft, then screeched to a halt at the bottom. "Oh, hi, Randy. Nice to see you again. Bye!" Turning, she scampered back up the steps and disappeared as quickly as she had come.

"I'm afraid my daughter's manners leave something to be desired," said Nick, frowning after her ruefully. He turned back to find Randy still waiting on the porch. "Then again, I haven't done much better, have I?" He stepped back and opened the door wide. "Won't you come in?"

"Thank you." Randy followed him inside, taking a quick look around as he closed the door behind them. The house had few interior walls, and the room she faced was an anomaly, managing to be large and yet cosy, all at the same time. Huge, plate glass windows and a cathedral ceiling high above them gave the impression of soaring space, while outsized furnishings in dark woods and muted earth tones created an atmosphere that was warm and cheery.

"Well," said Nick, coming up beside her. "This is a surprise. As you can see, I'm not exactly dressed for the occasion. If you wouldn't mind excusing me for just a second?"

"Of course." Randy nodded quickly. All of a sudden she had the distinct impression she'd made a terrible mistake. He looked so uncomfortable, it was almost a relief to watch him walk away.

What was she doing here, Nick wondered. He strode down the hall to his bedroom and pulled on the first thing that came to hand, an old red polo shirt whose alligator logo had long since fallen off and been lost. His movements jerky, he reached around and tucked in the long tails.

She was the last person he'd expected to find showing up on his doorstep. The last person he wanted to find there! Hadn't he spent the last four days trying to convince himself that things would be better for all concerned if he didn't see her again?

The whole situation was simply impossible. He'd realized that after the long, frustrating afternoon they'd spent together the previous Sunday. How many times during those hours had he longed to reach out and tangle his fingers through her silken hair, to touch the creamy skin of her shoulders and throat, to feel the warmth of her lips moving beneath his own?

Nick drew in his breath in a ragged, agonized groan. Instead, he'd had to content himself with acting like a damned eunuch. And all because of the sobering presence of his young, impressionable daughter. Not that he hadn't wanted Wendy there with them, Nick told himself quickly. The situation certainly wasn't her fault.

Indeed, if anything, it was his. He'd known from the first moment he'd laid eyes on Randy Wade that she was going to be trouble. Even that prickly defensiveness she'd aroused in him at their first meeting hadn't been enough to keep him away. No, if he'd had any sense at all, he'd have started running right then, and never stopped.

With any luck, Nick thought grimly, it might still not be too late. So she had come to his house to see him. So what? He would simply have to explain, as kindly but as firmly as possible, that as much as he was attracted to her, their involvement, such as it had been, was over.

Nick swore irritably under his breath. Hell, he thought, leaving his room and slamming the door behind him. How did you tell a woman you liked her too much to risk seeing her again? The whole thing sounded insane!

He found her in the living room, gazing out the large window that overlooked the back yard.

Sensing his presence, Randy turned as Nick entered the room. In the time while he was gone, she'd regained her composure, and now she was ready to confront him calmly and directly.

"Can I offer you something to drink?" Nick asked, crossing the room to a small bar in the corner. A little dutch courage never hurt anybody, he thought. Anything to make the job that had to be done a little easier.

"No thank you." Randy shook her head, her eyes following his long, lithe stride. If anything, he looked more tense now than he had when he left the room. Well, if she was the cause of his nervousness, thought Randy, she wouldn't stay around to bother him for long.

"Actually," she said. "I didn't mean for you to have to entertain me this evening. There's something I have to ask you. As soon as you've answered my question, I'll be on my way."

Nick paused in the act of pouring himself a stiff whiskey. "Shoot," he said, "I'm all yours."

Briefly Randy's eyes flickered toward the stairs, as she wondered whether or not Wendy could overhear them. Then she shrugged slightly. As far as secrecy went, the damage was already done anyway.

"As you may recall," she began stiffly, his wariness beginning to have an effect on her as well, "we discussed once or twice the importance of keeping my identity as Aunt Miranda a secret."

On the other side of the room, Nick raised the half full tumbler to his lips and took a quick gulp.

"Somehow it seems that the word has gotten out." Was it her imagination, Randy wondered, or did he actually seem to grow paler beneath his tan? "The people I work with at the newspaper had no idea how it might have happened. Since you're the only other person who was privy to that information, I can't help but wonder if perhaps you had something to do with it?"

"Well..." Nick grimaced slightly, his thoughts flying back to the conversation he had had with his daughter the previous Sunday. Damn, he'd been so sure she wouldn't give him away! "To tell the truth..." his voice faltered, then died away entirely. How was he ever going to explain his way out of this one?

"Damn it, Nick!" Randy cried, knowing that her fears had been confirmed by his silence. "How could you? You have no idea the amount of trouble you've caused me!"

"Would you believe me, if I tell you that it was an accident?"

Randy frowned uncertainly. At the moment, she had no idea what to believe. But now that he'd confirmed her suspicions, she could no longer ignore the doubts that had plagued her all throughout the long afternoon. All too clearly she remembered the way he had denigrated her job at their first meeting, calling her a trouble maker and berating her for sticking her nose in where it didn't belong. If he really thought so poorly of what she did, what better way to undermine her chances for success than by giving her identity away?

She'd told him how important Aunt Miranda's anonymity was, Randy mused grimly. No matter how strongly he denied it, surely something of that magnitude couldn't have simply slipped out by accident. What kind of fool did he take her for anyway?

Randy closed her eyes briefly, fighting a sharp shaft of pain. She'd been so sure that the rapport building between them had meant something, that the feelings they shared were stronger than any petty need for revenge generated by that letter she'd written to his daughter. Obviously she had been wrong.

"Randy, listen to me."

Setting down his drink, Nick strode quickly across the room. He had watched the rapid play of emotion across her face, and hadn't liked what he'd seen one bit. She didn't believe him, dammit! Good Lord, did she really think he would betray her confidence like that on purpose?

Reaching out, he wrapped his fingers around her upper arms. She stiffened beneath his grasp, and he found he had to resist the impulse to shake her. "I know what you're thinking," he said quickly. "And it isn't true at all. Here," he said, moving toward the couch, "sit down for a minute and I'll explain what happened."

Randy sank down beside him on the couch. "Go on."

"Last weekend, after Wendy and I took you home, she and I had a talk. She was going on and on about how much fun she'd had at the polo match, and about how good a listener you were and..." Nick shrugged helplessly. Even as he formed it, the excuse sounded lame. "And without thinking, I guess I blurted out something about how you were obviously used to listening to other people's problems."

Watching her face closely for any sign of forgiveness, Nick managed a rueful smile. "Unfortunately, giving a teenager the slightest inkling that you've said something you shouldn't is like handing a dog one end of a bone. Neither one will let go until they've dragged the whole thing out of you."

Numbly, Randy nodded. "I see."

"No," Nick rasped harshly. "I don't think you do." He wasn't getting through to her all. "I made Wendy promise that she wouldn't tell a soul. I believed her when she said that your secret was safe. Obviously that was my second mistake."

"Obviously," Randy agreed dryly.

Irrationally, Nick felt his anger begin to grow. How dare she sit there so coolly and calmly like some damn duchess and pass judgement on him? He'd admitted he was wrong, what more did she want?

"Now listen here," he began. "I'm sorry if this has inconvenienced you in any way—"

"Inconvenienced me?" Randy gasped.

All at once the numbing lethargy that had descended upon her fell away, replaced instead by a surging swell of anger that sent her leaping to her feet. She couldn't believe her ears! He was treating this whole thing and the effect it had on her life as though it was a minor annoyance of no real consequence, a nuisance that would blow over in time.

"Inconvenienced me?" she repeated incredulously. Propping her hands on her hips, she glared down at him furiously. "I'll tell you what this little mistake of yours has done. It has changed my entire life, and not for the better!

"This is a small town Nick, and news travels fast. Now that the word is out who Aunt Miranda really is, I've been besieged by phone calls at home, and deluged by suggestive letters at the office. Your little slip has turned me into a laughingstock among my peers. They're taking bets on what outrageous thing will happen next. Why, do you know I've had six proposals of marriage in the last four days alone?"

Some small gurgle of sound alerted her, and Randy looked down at Nick to find that his frame was shaking with silent laughter.

"Don't you dare laugh at me!" Randy fumed. "This isn't funny at all!"

"Of course not," Nick managed weakly. His expression was one of polite interest. "Did you say *six* marriage proposals?"

Curtly, Randy nodded. Frowning, she began to pace back and forth across the room. "And that isn't even the half of it! The whole thing has caused such a furor that even my managing editor has noticed what's going on. He called me into his office this afternoon and told me he wasn't sure how much longer the column could continue to run under the present conditions—that his paper valued serious journalism, not petty sensationalism."

Randy swallowed the lump that had risen suddenly in her throat. "He said my column was turning his newspaper into an object of ridicule, and that if this whole thing didn't blow over soon, he was going to have to take serious steps to remedy the situation."

"Oh Randy," Nick said softly, realizing for the first time the depth of her dilemma. "I am sorry."

Abruptly Randy stopped in her tracks, then slowly turned to face him. "Are you Nick?" she asked intently. "Are you really?"

"Of course I am." Nick frowned. "I never meant for anything like this to happen. Surely you know that."

"No," Randy said slowly. "I don't. And that's precisely the problem."

Nick glanced up sharply. "What's that supposed to mean?"

Randy heard the anger in his tone, but was past the point of caring. "You told me yourself what you thought of my job," she said scathingly, "and as I'm sure you recall, it wasn't very complimentary. Well now you may have done me out of that job, Nick, and yet you want me to believe that the whole thing came about purely by accident?"

"No," Nick said grimly. "That's not what I want you to believe. It's the truth."

"Of course." Turning away from him, Randy sighed deeply. As quickly as it had come, the fight seemed to have gone out of her, leaving her feeling empty and defeated. What did it really matter how this whole mess had come about, she thought. The damage had been done, and there was no going back to the way things had been before. Not in her job, and not in her relationship with Nick.

He moved so softly that she didn't hear him come up behind her, so she started slightly when his hands came to rest on her shoulders. "Is there anything," he said, and she felt the warmth of his breath rustle through her hair, "anything at all, that I can do to help?"

What she really wanted, Randy realized, was to turn around and bury herself in the warmth and comfort of his arms, to put aside her worries in the solace of his embrace. But that wouldn't solve anything. Indeed, she mused, in the long run, it would only make things worse. If she was going to break with Nick, it must be done quickly and cleanly. And now.

Hating the step she was about to take, but knowing it had to be done, Randy shrugged his hands away. "No," she said, her stance rigid as she twisted out of his grasp. "I think you've already done more than enough."

Slamming the front door behind her gave her no satisfaction at all.

The first thing Nick did after Randy left was pour himself a stiff drink. He carried the whiskey-filled tumbler into his den and sat down in an overstuffed leather armchair to sip at it thoughtfully.

She hadn't believed him, Nick mused. Not for a minute. But then again, why should she? Randy was right in saying that he didn't approve of her column. He didn't. Experience had taught him to know better. But as to the lady herself, now that was another matter entirely.

Nick shook his head slowly. What was it about her? he wondered, then grinned. Well obviously, there was the physical thing. But even beyond that, there was something about Randy Wade that drew him like a magnet. Her warmth maybe, and her openness—that easy affection with which she seemed to reach out and embrace the whole world.

In his whole life, he'd never met anyone quite like her before. Then again, Nick realized, in his early wild years, caring was one of the last things he'd looked for in a woman. No, he'd had something else in mind entirely. By the time he'd grown up enough to realize what love truly was, he'd been married to June—June who allotted her affections the way a scientist rewarded rats for running through a maze—doling them out and withdrawing them at will, depending on her assessment of his performance.

Then Wendy had come along and everything had changed. She'd become the center of all that was good in his life, and the focus of his unflagging devotion. He'd made a lot of mistakes in his youth, but they were behind him now. Nothing and no one, he had vowed, would ever come between him and his daughter.

And until now, nothing had, thought Nick. Indeed, nothing had even come close until a tawny-eyed vixen had stormed into his life and turned his carefully ordered existence upside down. In the beginning, he'd tried fighting her, and that hadn't worked. Then, this past week he tried ignoring her, and that hadn't done any better. As soon as he'd seen her at his door this evening, he'd realized just how much he missed the warmth and caring that were so much a part of her presence.

Nick frowned wryly. From all appearances, where Randy Wade was concerned, there was only one solution. He'd simply have to batten down the hatches and ride out the storm...and hope that he was still afloat by the time the ride was over.

Sipping once more at his drink, Nick smiled at the fanciful image. He supposed the first thing he'd have to do was get this whole Aunt Miranda mess straightened out. And he could start that right now, by giving Wendy one hell of a talking to....

The sound of someone knocking on the front door intruded on his thoughts, and Nick glanced up in surprise. Randy? he wondered. Was it possible she had come back? Setting down his drink on the side table, he leaped up and strode out to the front hall.

As he emerged from the den, Wendy came barreling down the stairs at top speed and he caught her in his arms and swung her away to avoid the inevitable collision.

"Dad!" Wendy gasped, looking none too pleased to see him. "What are you doing here?"

"I live here," Nick said dryly. "Remember?"

Wendy grimaced. "All I meant was that you didn't have to come out and answer the door. It's for me." Edging away, she placed herself between him and the door.

"Are you sure?" asked Nick, watching her machinations with a decidedly suspicious eye.

"Of course," Wendy replied blithely. "I told you earlier that a friend was coming over to listen to records with me, didn't I?"

"Yes." Nick frowned slightly, remembering. "I guess you did." He waited as his daughter reached for the knob, but still did not open the door. "Well," he said finally, "aren't you going to let her in?"

"Well, you see..." Wendy said slowly. "That's just it. This friend I told you about isn't exactly a her..."

Nick cleared his throat irritably. "Then what exactly is she?" Reaching around her, he grasped the knob and opened the door himself.

"Ahh," he said to himself, surveying the earring spangled boy dressed in a bright orange jumpsuit who waited on his front step. "I see we're not sure."

"Daddy!" Wendy wailed, her distress obvious.

"Good evening, sir." The boy smiled, cheerfully oblivious to Nick's displeasure.

"Not so far," Nick muttered audibly under his breath.

"Daddy, meet Eddie Grant," Wendy interjected quickly. "Eddie, this is my father." She waited for Nick to move back out of the way. When he didn't, she shrugged at Eddie in confusion. "Daddy," she said, laying a hand on his arm, "do you think Eddie might come in?"

"That depends," Nick replied easily, leaning against the doorjamb and still blocking the entrance, "on what he intends to do after he comes in."

"We're going to listen to records," Eddie announced pointing to the two albums he held tucked under his arm. "I have the newest by Duran Duran."

Nick's eyebrows lifted as he turned to face his daughter. "On your stereo?"

"Well..." Wendy shrugged. "Yes, I guess so."

"Your stereo is in your bedroom," Nick pointed out unnecessarily.

"That's all right," Eddie interjected cheerfully. "I don't mind."

"Well, I do!" Nick roared, and immediately regretted the outburst.

This was turning out to be one hell of a night. First the fight with Randy, and now this. Not to mention the fact that he still hadn't had a chance to have it out with Wendy for betraying his trust. And now to make matters worse, this...this...young punk thought he was going to make himself at home in his daughter's bedroom. Over his dead body, he was!

At another time, Nick realized, he might have told himself that Eddie didn't look nearly so bad as some he'd seen. Another time, he might have suggested that they use the stereo in the living room instead. He might have even controlled himself not to spy on them more than once or twice. But tonight control, as Nick was rapidly finding out, was a commodity he had precious little of.

"Daddy!" Wendy wailed. "What's the matter with you?"

"I'll tell you what's the matter," Nick said grimly. "No daughter of mine is going to lock herself away in her bedroom with a boy who looks like that!"

"What's the matter with the way I look?" asked Eddie, gazing down over his attire as if to make sure that it hadn't changed since the last time he'd checked.

Ignoring him, Wendy concentrated on placating her father instead. "But we were only going to listen to records."

"That," Nick said succinctly, "is what they all say."

"All who?" asked Eddie, and once again was ignored.

"We were, really," Wendy insisted, sticking out her lower lip in a pout. "I promise!"

"That won't wash with me, young lady," said Nick, looking down at her sternly. "At the moment it seems your promises mean precious little."

Wendy paled visibly, and Nick knew she realized what he was referring to. "Listen," she said, turning to Eddie, who was still standing on the step. "Now isn't really a good time. Maybe you'd better go."

He shrugged amiably. "All right doll, if that's what you want, I'm gone." Turning away, he hopped down the steps, climbed into his car and drove off down the drive.

Wendy watched until he'd disappeared from sight then, glaring at her father, she slammed the door so loudly that the windows rattled. Without another word, she turned and flounced away up the stairs.

Standing by himself in the front hall, Nick frowned. He hoped that things didn't go on like this much longer. That front door of his was never going to be able to stand the strain.

Later that evening, Randy put down the book she was reading when the doorbell rang. Now what? she wondered. After the day she'd had, she'd wanted nothing more than a little peace and quiet. That and the chance to lose herself in the plot of Dick Francis's latest thriller. Striding to the door, she threw it open irritably.

"All right, I give up," Nick announced. He was standing on the front porch, his hands held out, palms up in a gesture of surrender. Without waiting for an invitation, he walked past her and into the living room.

"What do you mean you give up?" Randy asked, frowning in confusion as she hurried after him. "Nick, what are you doing here?"

"Trying to regain my sanity, I think," he muttered succinctly, glancing around the small room. "Do you have any coffee?"

"Yes, of course," Randy replied automatically. "It's in the kitchen."

"Good." He crossed the room, and disappeared through the doorway, leaving Randy staring after him.

Now what on earth was she supposed to make of this?

She heard the sound of cabinet doors opening, then slamming shut; and in less than a minute, he'd reappeared, clutching a mug of steaming, black coffee before him as though it were a lifeline.

"Is there something I can do for you?" Randy inquired archly, watching as he sat down and made himself comfortable on the couch. "Or is this a solo performance?"

"Actually there is," Nick replied amiably. So amiably that Randy could cheerfully have socked him. He patted the plump cushion beside him. "You can come over here and sit down beside me. I think we need to talk."

Randy decided to do as she was told. After all, what choice did she have? The big lug had obviously settled in for the duration. Angry as she was at him, there didn't seem to be any hope of making him budge. And she couldn't very well go storming out of her own house.

"There," said Nick, draping an arm over her shoulder companionably. "That's much better."

"Nick." Randy sighed in exasperation. "Tell me what this is all about. Surely you didn't come here just to drink my coffee and…and…" She gestured uncertainly at his hand, which seemed to be inching slowly down her shoulder in the direction of her breast.

"Cop a feel?" Nick supplied easily. "No, of course not. But now that you mention it…"

"Nick Jarros!" Randy squealed. Grabbing the offending hand, she place it determinedly back in his lap.

"Sorry," said Nick, not sounding so in the least. "Just trying to interject a little levity into the situation."

"What situation?" Randy demanded suspiciously.

"The one we acted out earlier where you yell at me, and I yell at you, and then we both go off to our separate corners to sulk."

Randy stared at him incredulously. "Don't you think you're simplifying matters just a little?"

"Not at all," said Nick. Leaning forward, he set down his mug on the coffee table. When he turned once more to face her, Randy saw that his blue eyes were warm with caring. "I admit that I made a mistake, a big one, judging from all the problems it has caused you, and I'm genuinely sorry. But you've got to believe that I never intended for any of this to happen. When I told Wendy who you were—accidentally I might add—I had no idea what my carelessness might lead to."

"But—" Randy began, but Nick overrode her protest.

"I know what you're going to say and you're right. Ignorance is no excuse." He sighed wearily. "I guess all I can do is repeat how sorry I am for what happened, and hope that you'll forgive me."

Well, thought Randy, there it was, the choice she'd been deliberating all evening. Did she hold fast to her anger, knowing what a convenient buffer it would provide against a man to whose attractiveness she was becoming all too susceptible? Or did she allow herself to believe that the slip truly had been an accident, and by doing so, accept responsibility for the consequences that might follow?

It was a dangerous dilemma, she thought, one with risks to be weighed on either side. If she turned Nick away now, that would be the end of it. She would safeguard her emotions as she had learned to do in the past, taking no chances on being hurt.

But was safety really what she wanted, Randy mused. Always before, she had thought so. But now, with this man, she wasn't so sure. When she was with Nick, for the first time in her life she had caught glimpses of her dreams—visions of a rare and shining place where she was warm and cared for, and needed. Somewhere, deep down inside, she had begun to suspect that he was the man who could make the magic happen. Knowing that, how could she possibly send him away?

"So it was Wendy all along who proved my undoing," Randy mused aloud, stalling for time.

Nick nodded. "She and I have already had it out. She realized what she did was wrong, and she's planning to apologize the next time she sees you."

Randy smiled wanly. "I'll try not to be too hard on her."

Reaching out, Nick gathered both of her hands in his. "How about her father?" he asked softly. "Is he forgiven too?"

Slowly, recognizing the magnitude of the step she was about to take, Randy nodded. Immediately Nick's face lit with a smile. He gazed down upon her with such intensity that for a moment, she simply forgot to breathe.

"But that doesn't mean I'm not still angry," she insisted, the huskiness of her voice in direct conflict with her words. Pulling her eyes away, she tried to remember the feeling of outrage that had fueled her earlier. It was no use. When he looked at her like that, she wanted nothing more than to curl up in his arms and purr like a contented kitten.

"I know," Nick murmured. "But if we try hard enough, maybe we can put that behind us. As far as we're concerned, for tonight the rest of the world, especially its teenagers doesn't even exist...."

Randy watched as if mesmerized as his hand came up to stroke the side of her cheek gently.

"Tonight, there is only you and me."

Randy had thought their last kiss had been special but now, in the space of a few short seconds, she learned the difference between merely special and truly rare. Then she had been hesitant, unsure of Nick and her reaction to him. Now she moved to meet him eagerly, her mouth opening naturally beneath him, then moving with him as the kiss deepened.

Inching forward on the couch, Randy wound her arms around his waist, drawing him close and then closer still, surrounding him with her warmth. A soft sigh drifted between them, and she recognized it as her own.

"You know," Nick whispered, drawing back slightly, "for someone so small, you pack quite a punch."

"Small?" Randy laughed in a choked voice. Certainly no one had ever called her that before!

Yet in Nick's arms, she could almost believe it was true. Despite the passion that flowed between them, he held her carefully, almost reverently, as though she was a rare and fragile blossom to be coddled and protected. The magic was beginning to happen all over again, she realized. Despite her earlier misgivings, for the first time in her life, she felt not only cherished, but also truly safe.

"Nick, I—"

They both jumped at the same time, then looked at each other quizzically as the doorbell pealed shrilly.

"Don't tell me you were expecting someone else," Nick growled. His hands released her, and she rose unsteadily to her feet.

"No, of course not. I have no idea who..." As Randy drew open the door her voice slowly faded away.

A boy of perhaps fifteen with short, sandy-brown hair and thick wire-rimmed glasses was waiting on the step. "Aunt Miranda?" he said, smiling brightly. "I've come to talk to you."

"Here?" Randy gasped, too shocked to form a viable protest. "Now?" She turned helplessly to Nick and saw the thunderclouds that had begun to gather on his face.

"Sure, why not?" the boy asked as he let himself in. "No time like the present. That's what I always say." He strolled into the living room, his hands braced casually in the back pockets of his jeans. "Hey," he said, throwing a cheery wave in Nick's direction, "how's it going?"

Scowling, Nick threw up his hands in exasperation. She'd been put on this earth to torment him, that's what the problem was! God had looked down and said to himself, "Good old Nick looks pretty complacent these days. Let's send him something that will really shake him up!"

The trouble was, he couldn't decide who he was more furious at…Aunt Miranda, himself, or this grinning idiot of a teenage boy. Only one thing was clear. The way things were going, by the time he finally succeeded in getting Randy Wade all to himself, he'd probably be too old to do anything about it.

"That's it," he snapped, rising from the couch. "I'm leaving."

"Nick, wait!" Randy followed him across the room to the door. "This will only take a minute."

"Hey, no hurry," said the boy. "I've got all the time in the world."

"Not him," Randy snapped, spinning around to glare at him furiously. "You!"

Even before there was time to turn back around, the sound of the front door being softly closed alerted her to the fact that it was too late and Nick had gone.

"Damn!" Randy swore, her hands balling into fists at her sides.

So much for the magic.

Seven

Dear Aunt Miranda,

You're not going to believe what happened! The other night my parents asked me to babysit for my little sister while they went out to eat. Since it was a Saturday night and I had a date, I asked them if my boyfriend could come over to our house instead. They know him and like him a lot, so they said it was okay.

Well, I put my sister to bed and then he and I got to, you know, fooling around downstairs on the living-room couch. Somehow we lost track of the time. Either that, or they didn't bother with dessert. Anyway, they came home early, and found us in what you might call a sort of compromising position.

Were they ever livid! They threw my boyfriend out of the house, and they've forbidden me to ever see him again. Aunt Miranda, what we were doing wasn't really so bad, at least not when two people care about each other the way we do. Besides, it's not as if we were going all the way, or anything (if we had, they probably would have just killed us on the spot!)

I can't live without my boyfriend, and I know he feels the same way about me. Please write back quick and tell us what to do!

Signed,
Caught in the Act

Dear Caught,

Unfortunately you're writing to me a little late. If you had asked sooner, I would have told you that if you felt you had to do whatever it was you were doing, for God's sake, don't do it on the living-room couch! Now, however, the damage is already done.

I'm sure your parents feel just as bad about what happened as you do, but the upshot is that you have lost their trust, and now you are going to have to work very hard at regaining it. For starters, I would give them a little while to cool off (and hopefully forget the graphic details of what they saw). Then I would begin by asking them if you can entertain your boyfriend at home *when they are there* to act as chaperones. Needless to say, there had better not be any funny business going on!

I know it's hard, but you are both going to have to be on your best behavior. Everyone makes

mistakes, and you are going to have to convince
them that you've put yours behind you. Show
them that you are willing to earn their trust, and
with any luck, in time, they will come to respect
your relationship with your boyfriend as they
once did. Good luck. I'll be rooting for you!

Signed,
Aunt Miranda

To Randy's relief, Nick's temper tantrum, as she
privately called it, didn't last long. When he called the
next day and apologized, then asked her out for Saturday evening, she accepted eagerly.

Unsure of what the plans were, she dressed casually and was pleased, when she greeted Nick at the
door, to see that he had done the same. After ascer-
taining their mutual love of Chinese food, they
hopped in the car and were on their way. It wasn't until halfway through a shared dinner of wonton soup,
moo shoo pork, and Mandarin chicken, that Randy
found out what form of entertainment he had in mind
for the rest of evening.

"You may think I was a bit curt with you the other
evening, but that was nothing compared to the way I
came down on Wendy," Nick informed her. He explained about his daughter's aborted date, adding at
the end, "To tell the truth, that kid, Eddie, didn't
really seem all bad. Maybe if I had given him half a
chance..."

Randy nodded, picturing the scene in her mind. "I
can just imagine what happened," she said, spearing
a piece of the sweet chicken and putting it into her
mouth. "But if you don't mind my asking, what does
that have to do with us?"

"Well," Nick said slowly, "I wanted to make it up to her somehow, so I told her she could go out with Eddie if she really wanted. They made plans for this evening..."

Randy's eyebrows lifted quizzically. Maybe that little lecture she'd given him at the polo match hadn't gone for nothing, after all.

"It wasn't until he came to pick her up that I found out where they were going..." Nick's voice trailed away once more.

"And?" Randy prompted. This was like pulling teeth!

"And—" he finished in a rush—"as it turns out he's taking her to a drive-in movie. I was thinking maybe we'd like to go along too."

His comment drew a startled glance, then slowly Randy began to laugh. "Do you mean to tell me," she sputtered incredulously, "that you want us to double-date with your daughter at a drive-in?"

"No, of course not." Nick frowned, looking not the slightest bit amused. "We'll be in two separate cars—"

"I should hope so," Randy muttered, picturing the streamlined Ferrari they'd left parked out front.

"And we'll park several rows away. Why, Wendy will never even know we're there."

This was coming from a man who was supposed to be loosening the restraints he'd placed on his daughter!

"You mean you hope she'll never know. Nick Jarros, you're planning on spying on her, aren't you?"

Nick shifted uncomfortably in his chair. "Not exactly. It's just that I'd feel much better about the whole thing if I knew she wasn't entirely on her own."

"You might," said Randy. "But how do you think Wendy is going to feel? She'll think that you don't trust her."

"It's not Wendy that I'm worried about. But Eddie is another matter. No boy takes a girl to a dark, secluded drive-in movie unless he's up to something."

Randy gazed at him consideringly. "And I suppose you ought to know?"

"Yes, damn it!" Nick signaled for the waiter and quickly paid the check. "And no daughter of mine is going to get into that kind of trouble while I'm around to prevent it."

By the time they were ensconced once more in the little sportscar, speeding toward the Outdoor Theatre two towns away, Randy had begun to see the humor in what admittedly had to be an absurd situation. Good grief, she thought, leaning her head back against the plush leather seat. She couldn't even remember the last time she'd been to a drive-in. She'd probably been a teenager herself at the time.

Randy giggled under her breath. The two of them were going to look like a couple of overaged swingers, trying to relive the glory of their youth. Even if they somehow managed to lay low in that teenage crowd, the Ferrari was going to stick out like a sore thumb! Nick must be crazy to think he could pull this off without Wendy finding out about it. And she was probably equally crazy for going along for the ride.

When they arrived, Randy read the movie title on the flashing marquee as they took their place in line and knew her evening was complete.

"*A Teenage Rock Star in Outer Space*?" she said, giggling delightedly. "Is that really what you're taking me to see?"

"It looks that way, doesn't it?" Nick stared at the sign for a long moment before turning to grin at her in the flickering light. "I never even stopped to think about the show itself. Do you think you'll be able to manage to sit through it?"

Seeing the concerned look on his face, Randy's laughter slowly died. All at once she became aware of the cosy intimacy generated by their surroundings. For the first time she realized that for the next two hours, they would be locked together in that small cocoon. Set apart from the rest of the world, they would be decidedly, and deliciously, alone.

It was, she decided, with a thrill of reckless anticipation, rather an enticing thought! Gazing at Nick across the small distance that separated them, she realized that she was very much looking forward to whatever the evening might bring. "Don't worry about me," she said brightly. "I'll be just fine."

As the line moved forward, they paid for their tickets, then drove into the crowded lot. "There they are, that's Eddie's car," said Nick, nodding toward an old white Ford that had taken a place near the back of the lot. Cruising down the aisle, he pulled into a vacant space two rows further back near the concession stand. "We should be able to keep an eye on them from here."

"Anything you say, Sherlock," Randy murmured, and Nick shot her a dry glance. Ignoring him, she squinted in the direction of the white Ford. "But just what exactly are we looking for? I don't know about you, but I can't see much of anything."

Nick had a look for himself. "Well," he said finally, frowning as he cocked his head from one side to the other. "I have to admit the view isn't perfect, but I think I can see two heads sitting up in the front seat.

All we have to do is keep an eye on them and make sure they don't go anywhere.''

"Aye aye.'' Randy tossed him a jaunty salute. "I'll do my best.''

As the large screen before them flickered to life, Nick reached out and took the audio box off its stand, hooking it onto the side of the car. "If we're going to watch, we may as well listen,'' he said with a grin as the first tinny strains of a strident rock-and-roll song filtered into the car.

"You're enjoying this, aren't you?

"Of course,'' said Nick, settling back comfortably in his seat. "Aside from anything else, it brings back all sorts of memories.''

"Oh?'' Randy's brows lifted. Smiling, she shifted in her seat to face him. "Tell me more.''

"Hey, would you look at that!'' All at once Nick became totally absorbed in the drama on the screen. "The mother ship is about to land!''

"Big deal,'' Randy scoffed, seeing through his ploy. "Once you've seen one of these rock-and-roll space epics, you've seen them all.''

"And have you?'' Nick asked curiously. "Seen another one, I mean?''

"Sure.'' Randy nodded. "Last year when *Futuristic Flames* came out, I got all sorts of letters from kids whose parents wouldn't let them see it. They wanted an opinion, and the only way I could give them that was to go and find out for myself what the movie was all about.''

"And did you wind up agreeing with the teenagers or with their parents?''

"Both,'' Randy replied with a smile as she remembered. "I agreed with the parents that the movie was trash and a total waste of time. But I also agreed with the kids that if they wanted to see it, there was nothing in there so morally offensive that they ought to be kept away."

"How very diplomatic," Nick taunted her lightly.

"Oh yeah?" Randy snorted. "I should think you of all people would know that I don't go out of my way to please everybody. I tell the truth, and if anyone doesn't like it, then they can go somewhere else for an opinion."

"And what," Nick asked, waving toward the screen, "is your opinion of our current offering?"

"Do you really want to know?"

Nick nodded, and Randy turned to study the screen where several guitar-toting teenagers, dressed in neon-colored futuristic garb had just entered a bar ruled by a space creature who looked like a quivering blob of lime jello. "If it's not the silliest movie I've ever seen, it's certainly trying hard to come close."

"Is that so?" said Nick, rising quickly to the movie's defense. "Then maybe you just don't recognize escapist fiction at its best. I'll have you know some of the best moments of my youth were spent in just such a place as this, watching movies that probably had no more redeeming value than this one does."

Randy grinned wickedly. "But the question is, were you really watching the movie, or are those memories of yours of something else entirely?"

To her delight, Nick reddened slightly. "Well, to tell the truth..." He shrugged helplessly, and they broke up laughing together.

"Just as I suspected," Randy said with a nod. "Nobody in his right mind would watch that!"

Her giggles escalated as she glanced at the screen once more. Now, some sort of fight had broken out, and the intrepid heroes were using their space-age instruments as weapons.

"I can't believe it!" she squealed, her voice breaking on choked laughter. "Now they're trying to guitar that poor jello mold to death. Why doesn't somebody just hand them a couple of spoons and be done with it?"

Nick glanced apprehensively at the other cars that surrounded them, his good humor fading. "Shhh!" he warned nervously. "Not so loud. People are staring!"

For his sake, Randy made a concerted effort to quell the laughter that was bubbling merrily in her breast. Schooling her features into some semblance of calm, she tried concentrating on the screen. It took less than a minute, however, for her to realize how big a mistake that was.

Giggling once more under her breath, she shifted her gaze away. One look at the somber expression on Nick's face should have been enough to stop her giggling, but to Randy's dismay, it had the opposite effect. The laughter that rumbled deep in her chest finally escaped to reverberate throughout the small car.

As if the movie itself wasn't bad enough, she thought, giggling helplessly. Now she was going to be expected to sit through it with a man whose face looked as though it should have been carved on Mount Rushmore. Couldn't he see how absurd this whole thing was? Not to mention the harebrained undercover operation that had brought them here in the first place...!

"Randy, I'm warning you..." Nick rasped, glancing around desperately. "We're trying to maintain a low profile here!"

"I know," Randy choked out helplessly, "and I'm trying, I really am but...but..." She gestured toward the screen, then back toward him as though that explained everything, her voice dissolving once more into a cascade of giggles.

Watching her, Nick scowled irritably. Now what was he supposed to do? With all this noise, it was only a matter of time before somebody took a look into the car to see what was going on. And once these kids saw who they were...Nick groaned softly. He didn't even want to think about it!

Leaning across the hand brake that separated them, he ran one arm along the back of Randy's seat, circling her shoulder. With the other hand, he reach up and covered her mouth with his palm. Now the force of her muffled laughter shook them both.

"Oh for Pete's sake," Nick muttered. In a desperate situation, desperate measures were called for!

Slowly he drew her toward him across the seat. Randy watched, her eyes open wide and fixed unblinkingly on his as he lowered the palm that covered her mouth and leaned down to replace it with his lips. As if a hidden switch had been flipped deep inside, abruptly her laughter died.

"Nick?" she said softly, wonderingly.

"Shhh," he said again, shifting his torso in the seat so that she fit comfortably along his length. "Don't say a word."

As if she wanted to, thought Randy, lifting her face to his. Her hands came up, her fingers framing the bones of his jaw and guiding him to her. Then their mouths met in a heated union that drove all other thoughts from her mind.

Oh Lord, but it felt good. His lips were soft and warm upon hers, his tongue probing gently until she responded to its demand and opened her mouth to him. His small moan of satisfaction was swallowed between them as his tongue dipped inside to taste and savor.

Then it was Randy's turn to moan as he began a subtle stroking motion that awakened a heavy, throbbing response she felt deep in the pit of her stomach. Her hips shifted, her body arching mindlessly upward as it blossomed beneath his touch.

Their surroundings—the cramped front seats, the other cars that surrounded them—all faded to insignificance. Losing himself in the kiss, Nick was aware of nothing save the passion that coursed suddenly through his veins. What had started as no more than an expedient measure had now turned into something else entirely—a driving need whose force had caught him unaware, and whose pleasure-filled possibilities left him breathless.

Reaching down, Nick released the hand brake that stuck up like a rigid sentinel between their two seats, and pressed himself closer. He had tried to take things slowly, for his sake as well as hers. But Lord, he was only human! Just how human was becoming clearer and clearer by the moment. When she burst into flames beneath his hands, he knew he could hold back no longer.

His lips never left hers as Nick slipped one hand down along the side of Randy's body. Reaching beneath her to cradle her buttocks in his large palm, he lifted her up off the seat, then slid across the small space that separated them to settle himself beneath her.

Randy shivered slightly as he lowered her onto his lap and the skirt of her light, cotton dress rode up to tangle about her thighs. She felt the force of his desire proclaimed unashamedly against the curve of her hip, and her nerve endings heated and tingled, sparking with the fire that seemed to grow with each passing second.

Randy drew a deep, quivering breath and her breasts lifted, grazing the solid plane of his chest. As if the clothes between them didn't even exist, she felt the tangle of crisp hairs that curled beneath his shirt teasing her sensitive skin. Immediately her nipples hardened in response, jutting forward as Nick reached up to cup the full, heavy weight of her breast in his palm.

"So soft," he whispered roughly. "So very feminine."

His head lowered, his tongue darting out to find the sensitive peak beneath the fabric of her dress and bathe it with a gentle stroke. He growled softly, deep in his throat. The hand which circled her shoulders dipped lower, his fingers splaying open to span her back as he used the hold to press her to him.

Gentleness was forgotten as his tongue stroked her with a new and demanding fervor. His hand circled her breast holding it steady as he nestled against her. Then his mouth circled the nipple, bathing flesh and fabric both—sucking, tugging, pulling, until Randy strained against him, crying out sharply at the waves of sensation that crested within her.

She felt his need, a desperation almost, and responded to it instinctively, her fingers tunneling through his thick, dark hair, shaping themselves to the sides of his head so that she could hold him to her. The force of his desire reached out to something strong within her, awakening needs of her own that had been held too long in check.

Never had she felt so fulfilled, Randy thought with a shuddering sigh as her body hummed with the rightness of what was happening between them. Never before had she felt so very much a woman—a woman who was everything her man needed her to be.

"Tell me," Nick murmured, "tell me that you want me."

"I want you," Randy breathed. "I want you Nick, more than I have every wanted anything—"

Abruptly, a loud screech rent the air. Nick and Randy jerked apart guiltily then looked at each other in surprise as the source of the noise became clear. The sound box that Nick had fastened to the side of the car jiggled in its precarious spot, emitting one last squawk before dropping off the window to land with a loud clatter on the pavement below.

"What the hell...?" Nick swore vehemently, twisting around to see what had happened.

"Hey mister, do you realize your car's rolling?" A pair of bright, curious eyes leaned down to peer in the side window of the Ferrari, and immediately Randy recognized the boy as one whose girlfriend played on her team. "You must have forgotten to set the hand brake or something."

"Oh good Lord," Nick muttered.

He moved instinctively to shield Randy from the teenager's curious gaze as she hastily pulled the top of her dress up, and the bottom of her dress down. There was no way to hide the fact that she was sitting on his lap, however; nor the way the bodice, even when pulled back into place, clung to her breasts damply.

"Oh, wow..." the boy breathed softly, suddenly realizing what he'd interrupted. "Hey," he said, standing up and backing away hastily, "that's cool..."

"Whatcha up to Pete?" asked a second voice, and Nick cringed inwardly in recognition.

Oh no, he thought with a small groan, closing his eyes and praying that he was mistaken.

"What's the matter?" The voice continued, and Nick knew his prayers had gone unanswered. "Hey, does this guy realize he lost his squawk box?"

Pausing beside the car, Eddie leaned down to pick up the piece of missing equipment. "Well no wonder," he said, stretching the cable, and realizing that it wouldn't reach. He leaned down to peer in the window helpfully. "You're gonna have to back up if you want to listen…" His voice faded away as his eyes widened in surprise. "Mr. Jarros!"

"Hello Eddie," Nick said with as much dignity as he could muster under the circumstances.

"What are *you* doing here?" The boy's shock was clearly evident in his tone.

"We're here for the same reason you are," Nick growled, uncomfortably aware that Randy was still seated, rather provocatively, in his lap. Grimly he wondered whether he ought to slide out from under her or whether, given the present state of his arousal, that would only make matters worse. "To watch the movie."

"Sure," said Eddie, straightening quickly, "anything you say."

Beside him, his friend snickered loudly. "You must have quite a view from there." Nick heard him intone.

"Now wait just a minute!" Nick snarled. Grasping Randy by the shoulders, he twisted out from beneath her, slid back into the driver's seat and reached for the handle of the door. "This is not what it looks like—"

"Hey, no problem." Eddie shrugged breezily. "What you're doing in there is your business. I was just on my way to the concession stand for some popcorn." Grinning broadly, he began to back away. "I'd better be going. I'd hate to keep Wendy waiting for too long."

Chuckling together under their breath, the two boys walked away down the aisle. "And to think," Nick heard Eddie mutter, "he was worried about what *we* might get up to!" His face flushed with embarrassment as the two boys laughed once more.

"Nick?" Randy said questioningly. She reached out and placed one hand gently atop his arm. "Who was that boy? Did you know him?"

"That boy," Nick bit out succinctly, "was my daughter's date!"

"Oh no," Randy moaned, sympathy welling up within her.

Reaching for the key, Nick turned on the ignition. "I think I've seen enough for one evening," he said grimly, piloting the Ferrari quickly out of the lot. "And I know for damn sure that they have!"

Tires squealing a protest, they pulled out onto the road and roared away into the night.

They drove for several minutes in total silence, each lost in private contemplation of the scene that had just taken place.

Well, the cat was really out of bag now, Randy mused grimly. There was no way Wendy wasn't going to find out what her father had been up to. Just what would Eddie tell her, she wondered, cringing as she recalled what the boy must have seen.

Then again, thought Randy, Wendy was a big girl now, certainly much more mature than her father gave her credit for. In fact, she wouldn't be at all surprised if the teenager wasn't more upset at her father's spying on her, than that he'd been caught engaging in a little adult recreation. No, Randy mused thoughtfully, from what she knew of Wendy, the girl was mature enough to take something like that completely in her stride.

Which was more than could be said for her father, Randy decided, sneaking a peek at his stern visage out of the corner of an eye. Good Lord, he looked about ready to spit nails! So they'd been caught necking in a drive-in, so what? Worse things had happened. Why was Nick so upset?

"Hey," Randy said softly, turning in her seat to face him. "Are you all right over there?"

Nick's only reply was a barely audible grunt.

Undaunted, Randy tried again. "It's not the end of the world, you know." She eyed the speedometer as the Ferrari skidded around a curve. "Although it might be if you don't slow down a bit."

Flushing guiltily, Nick eased off the gas pedal.

"Why don't you tell me what's wrong," Randy said soothingly. "You're bound to feel better if we talk about it."

"I should think the answer to that is obvious!"

"Not to me it isn't," Randy said stoutly. "Are you really so worried about how Wendy might react? For God's sake, Nick, she knows you're a grown man. I imagine something like this won't faze her at all. In fact, I wouldn't be surprised if she and Eddie weren't sharing a good laugh over the whole thing right now."

"Is that what you think?" Nick demanded. Giving the wheel a sharp twist, he guided the Ferrari over to the side of the road and cut the motor. "That what happened back there tonight was funny?"

"No, of course not," Randy said quickly. "Although I can see how Wendy might think so. Surely she knows you're not a monk?

"If she does," Nick said grimly, "it certainly hasn't been because I've given her any graphic demonstrations of the fact." Moaning softly, he shook his head. "How can I help but be angry about what happened? I've always been so careful to try and set the best possible example for her, and now, in one moment of recklessness, I may have undone all the good that's gone before."

"Surely you don't really believe that," Randy said incredulously. "And if you do, I don't think you're giving your daughter enough credit. From what I've seen of Wendy, she is a mature, levelheaded girl who's more than capable of forming her own opinions of what's right and what's wrong. You may have dictated her moral code so far, but you're fast reaching the point where that's no longer possible. You're not going to have any choice but to let go; and to trust that the guidance you've given her already will lead her in the right direction."

Leaning back against the bucket seat, Nick sighed heavily. "I know what you're saying is true, but I can't help thinking that I haven't done enough. Damn it, she's just too young—"

"She's fifteen years old, Nick, and becoming more and more grown up every day. You've got to accept that and start treating her accordingly. She's not going to get into any trouble—"

"Maybe not on purpose," Nick muttered. "But accidents do happen. All you have to do is read the papers to know how many teenage pregnancies there are in this country every year."

Randy glanced up in surprise. "Is that what you're afraid of? That Wendy will get pregnant?"

"Yes!" Nick spat out harshly. His expression as he turned to face her was bleak. "That's *exactly* what I'm afraid of! Something like that changes a kid's life forever." He shook his head bitterly. "I should know. It happened to me."

Randy's eyes widened in startled surprise. She'd known from what he'd said that his marriage wasn't a happy one. Indeed, from the way he talked about this first wife, she'd often wondered what had prompted them ever to get married in the first place. Well, Randy thought with a sigh, now she knew.

"Do you want to talk about it?" she asked softly. Her hand made its way across the top of the seat to settle on his shoulder comfortingly. When he hesitated, she added, "I've been told I make a pretty good listener."

"There really isn't much to tell," Nick said with a shrug, pausing once more. Randy waited in silence until he was ready to continue. "When I was a kid, I guess I was what you might call a bit of a hell raiser. My parents weren't too big on discipline, and I ran pretty wild. By the time I reached my twenties, I had more than my share of fast times...more than my share of women too...." His voice trailed away as he looked down into Randy's eyes. "You don't have to hear about all this if you don't want to."

"No," Randy said truthfully. "I do. Please go on."

"I met June the same way I met most of my dates in those days—in a bar. I was impressed because she could hold her beer better than any girl I'd ever seen. She was impressed because I had the biggest motorcycle in town." Nick frowned bitterly. "Back then, it was enough. I guess up till that point I'd been lucky, but when I met June, my luck ran out. We'd only been going together a couple of months when she told me she was pregnant."

Randy winced, hearing the pain in his voice. The fingers that gripped his shoulder gave a reassuring squeeze.

"She told me she didn't want the baby—that if I gave her the money, she'd be happy to get rid of it. Can you imagine?" Nick said raggedly, shaking his head. "She wanted to get rid of our daughter as if she was nothing more than so much excess baggage."

"And then?"

"I guess you might say I sort of forced her to marry me. I promised her that I would change, that things would be different. And I did change. In fact, as it turned out that event was the pivotal point in my life. Before that, I was living in the fast lane, running in high gear and heading for nowhere. But after Wendy came along..." Nick's voice broke in remembered wonder. "The idea of having a baby, an actual living, breathing part of myself to care for, brought me around in a hurry."

"So then maybe things did work out for the best," Randy mused aloud, and Nick looked up sharply.

"Maybe, maybe not. Don't get me wrong—I could never regret bringing Wendy into the world, but look what's happened to her as a result of my mistake. She's spent virtually her entire life without knowing what it's like to have a mother. She never chose something like that, it was forced upon her."

"Choices," Nick said softly. His eyes found hers. "In the end, that's what it all comes down to. I want Wendy to have the freedom I never had—to choose her life's direction rather than having it thrust upon her by fate."

"Listen to yourself, Nick," Randy said gently. "Listen to what you're saying. You want your daughter to have her independence, but when it comes right down to it, you're the very person who's standing in her way."

"Maybe so," said Nick, his tone implacable. "But for now, that's the way things have to be."

Closing her eyes, Randy sighed softly. Were they forever destined to be at odds with each another? Mounting opposing campaigns where in the end both would inevitably lose? Building a relationship was difficult enough without trying to fit in the needs of a third person as well. Yet this time, they had no choice. There were so many ways she cared about Nick. But until they got this issue resolved, how could they even begin to think about themselves?

Drawing in a deep breath, Randy let it out slowly and took one last try at finding the words that would make him understand. "Don't you see, Nick," she said softly. "You've given Wendy so many things in the past fifteen years. Now it's time to give her one more gift—perhaps more precious than all the rest—your trust."

In the dim light of the front seat Randy saw Nick's eyes narrow thoughtfully. Had she gotten through to him this time, she wondered as the Ferrari pulled out onto the road and turned once more toward home. Had he truly heard—and understood—what she was trying to say? Only time would tell.

Eight

Dear Aunt Miranda,

A few weeks ago, I started going out with a girl that I thought was pretty special. Every time I saw her my knees got weak and I got all hot and breathless. My shirt would soak through with perspiration. I mean I really had it bad!

I was sure this was the real thing. It *had* to be love, I figured. What else could it be? I was ready to buy her a ring, go down on one knee and propose, the whole enchilada. Well, none of that ever happened. Before I had a chance, my mother decided that I wasn't looking so hot, and made an appointment for me with the doctor.

You'll never believe this, Aunt Miranda, but according to him, it wasn't true love at all. It turned out all I really had was the flu!

Well I'm better now, but I hope somebody else will be able to learn from my mistake. I'm still seeing my girlfriend, but she and I are taking things quite a bit slower now. Believe me, that suits me just fine!

Signed,
Saved by Medical Science

Dear Saved,

I'm glad to hear everything worked out for the best in the end, although you probably weren't too far off base when you got your symptoms confused. Greater minds than mine have pondered the existence of true love and failed to come up with an answer.

All I can say is, if you're lucky, you'll recognize what's really happening when the time comes. If not...well, I'd keep that doctor's number handy if I were you!

Signed,
Aunt Miranda

The next day was Sunday, and Randy was all set to spend a lazy day at home. Donning a brightly patterned bikini, she had just gone out into the backyard to do some gardening, when Nick's jeep roared up the driveway and pulled to a halt beside the house. She set down her tools and strolled around the side of the house in time to see him emerge from one side of the jeep and his daughter from the other.

"Perfect!" Wendy squealed, clapping her hands gleefully at Randy's appearance. "You're all ready."

"Ready for what?" Randy turned toward Nick questioningly. Her breath caught in her throat as she felt the full effect of the smoldering gaze he had trained upon her.

"Perfect indeed," he muttered softly. His blue eyes roamed slowly up and down over her scantily clad body, missing nothing from her long, tanned legs to her flat midriff, to her sun-warmed breasts, confined by only two small scraps of bright green material.

"Thank you, sir." Randy smiled prettily. To her surprise, she felt neither discomfort, nor embarrassment at his intimate perusal. For the first time that she could remember, there was no urge to slink away in shame, no compelling need to cover herself from curious eyes.

Instead Randy simply stood her ground and returned his look in full measure. She took in the way sun glinted off his dark hair, bringing out the bronze highlights in the unruly mass of curls; noted with approval the slim fit of his open-necked polo shirt, and the ragged pair of cut-off denims that adorned his hips. What a hunk, she mused dreamily.

"Why, for the beach, of course," Wendy cried enthusiastically, bringing her swiftly back to the present. "We're on our way there now. Daddy thought you might like to join us."

"That is," Nick interjected smoothly, "if you're not busy. With weather like this," he gestured at the clear sky above them, "Candlewood Lake is bound to be crowded, but somehow the opportunity seemed too good to miss."

"I'm not busy at all," Randy replied, grinning delightedly. "And I'd love to come. Let me just run inside and pull on a cover-up and I'll be right with you."

The trip to the lake took less than ten minutes. Upon their arrival, Wendy leaned up from the back seat to poke her head between them, directing Nick through the entire lot until she found just the spot she sought. The reason for her choice soon became apparent. Unpacking the car, Nick and Randy heard the first gleeful shouts as Wendy ran down onto the narrow beach and was greeted by a bevy of her friends.

"Wonderful," Nick groaned, lifting a heavy cooler full of cold drinks from the back of the jeep. "That's all we need." He turned to Randy, shaking his head apologetically. "You know, I'm beginning to think that daughter of mine has quite a devious streak. When she proposed spending a day at the beach this morning, she somehow neglected to mention who else might be coming."

"That's all right," Randy said lightly, following him down to the lake. "I don't mind at all. Besides, try to look on the bright side. Now we won't have to worry about Wendy being bored with nobody but a couple of old fogies like us around for company."

"Old fogies, eh?" Nick lifted one brow humorously. He spread out the large olive-drab army blanket he was carrying on the hot sand then straightened to face her, flexing his muscles teasingly. "Speak for yourself, madam. I, for one, am in the prime of my life!"

She wasn't about to dispute that, Randy thought, letting her gaze shift over his sun-bronzed body as he pulled his shirt over his head and tossed it down onto the blanket.

Tearing her eyes away from his bare chest she announced, "Time for a swim! Last one in buys lunch!" Unbuttoning her cover-up, Randy flung it down beside his shirt.

She beat him into the lake, but only just barely, running through the shallow water until the bottom dropped away and she dove into the clear depths beyond. She surfaced several moments later, holding back her head to skim the hair back off her face. Standing in chest-deep water, she found Nick floating on his back no more than a few feet away.

"You lose!" she chortled gleefully, splashing a handful of cold water up onto his exposed chest.

"Oh I don't know," Nick drawled. His feet dropped suddenly from sight as he rose to stand beside her. "I'd say that's all in how you look at things, wouldn't you?"

He was too close, thought Randy. So close that she could see the smooth texture of the sun-warmed skin that covered his broad shoulders; so close that her eyes couldn't help but follow the twisting descent of the rivulets of water that traced a path down the hair-matted planes of his chest; so close that the entire world seemed to consist of only the two of them and the heat that crackled between them like a live wire twisting on a hot summer street.

Helplessly, her eyes lifted to his.

"Ran—dy," Nick murmured softly, drawing out her name into two long, breathless syllables. "What am I ever going to do with you?"

It was then, in that moment, that she knew the answer to his question. He was going to make love to her. They were going to make love together. Not now, but soon, because all at once Randy knew that she had never wanted anything so much as she wanted to lie beside this man, her body complementing his, two halves forming a single whole as they moved together as one.

"Yes," she whispered roughly, her voice no louder than his.

Nick's eyes softened. No further words were needed, Randy realized. He knew exactly what she meant. His thoughts had mirrored hers; she could read the passion in his eyes. Slowly Nick backed away, careful not to touch her.

"I, er..." Randy stammered, then shrugged. "I guess I'll go back up to the beach."

Nick nodded. "I'll be along in a few minutes. I'm in no state to be seen right at the moment, if you know what I mean."

Randy smiled slowly at his predicament. The smile widened into a grin, then finally a full-fledged chuckle, releasing the last of the tension that hummed between them. "Don't be too long," she said back over her shoulder flippantly. "It's just about time for that lunch you owe me!"

After lunch—a meal of hot dogs and chili purchased from a concession stand at the end of the beach—Nick and Randy settled down side by side on the blanket to watch as Wendy and some of her friends erected a volleyball net in the sand.

"Ah, the boundless energy of youth," Randy sighed, sprawling out lazily in the warm sun. "Don't they realize how much nicer it is just to lie here and soak up the bennies?"

"Bennies?" Nick echoed quizzically as the boys finished securing the poles and began to stretch the net taut from one end to the other.

To his relief, both Eddie and his friend Pete had had the good grace not to mention the previous night's encounter. Indeed, he mused, he'd been quite surprised by their silence, steeling himself for the teasing he'd been sure was inevitable. Instead they'd handled the situation with a maturity he had not expected at all. They'd simply greeted him with the calm, quiet respect due Wendy's father and had gone on with the business of enjoying their day at the beach. To his continuing amazement, this afternoon's outing, which could have been quite awkward, had turned out to be a rather pleasant occasion all around.

"You know." Randy looked up, shading her eyes with her hand. "Bennies—beneficial rays?"

"Of course," Nick said wryly as though the answer was perfectly obvious. "I should have known. I guess that's another one of those teenage expressions that I always seem to be behind on?''

"Yup," Randy said smugly, closing her eyes once more. "You got it."

"Hey Mr. Jarros, you want to play?"

Nick looked up quickly in surprise. The volleyball net was secure and ready to go, and the teenagers grouped around it were gazing at him expectantly. "No, I don't think so," he said, amused by the invitation. "But thanks for asking."

"Ahh, come on," Wendy pleaded. Striding through the deep sand to the edge of the blanket, she grasped his hand, then braced backward to pull him to his feet. "You'll have fun. Besides, if you don't play, the teams won't be even, and then somebody else will have to sit out."

"Well," Nick said dubiously, "if you really need me..."

"We do!" A chorus of voices cried together.

Randy laughed as she sat up to watch. "Go on, Nick! It looks to me as though you've been drafted."

In no time at all, Nick found himself installed as the captain of a team whose members included both Wendy and Eddie, plus an assortment of other teenagers whose names he forgot almost as soon as they were given. Assessing their own strengths and weaknesses, the team chose their positions and the play began.

Lord, but I must be getting old, Nick thought, suppressing a small groan forty-five long, sweaty minutes later. The first game had just ended with his team winning by a narrow margin, and now the losers on the other side of the net were clamoring for a rematch.

Where on earth did they get all that energy? he wondered, thinking longingly of the six-pack of cold beer sitting waiting for him in the cooler. They couldn't possibly be serious about starting another game, could they? It turned out they could. Avoiding the laughter in Randy's gaze, Nick made his way resignedly to the front line and prepared to receive the serve.

This time the game was somewhat quicker, with the advantage in the end going to the other team.

"Best two out of three!" cried a young, pony-tailed girl, whose name Nick seemed to remember as Genie. A chorus of assent followed her declaration. Shaking his head and muttering inaudibly under his breath, Nick took up his position once more. He didn't care what they said next, this was definitely the last one.

It wasn't until the middle of that last game that Nick realized how well the teenagers played together as a team. Indeed, he thought with grudging admiration, they threw themselves into the effort with a determination and unflagging sense of enthusiasm that any team captain would be proud to call his own.

Granted it was only a game being played out on a sandy beach on a lazy Sunday afternoon, but still he couldn't help but notice how well the kids handled themselves. They gave direction and took it, all with the same easy companionability; calling out instructions to set up the best possible plays as the ball crossed the net time and time again.

Smiling to himself, Nick watched as Eddie set up a high, looping shot for Wendy's spike. Unexpectedly he found himself remembering the cut-throat competitiveness of his own youth and realized that for the second time that day, the boy had surprised him. Obviously not at all averse to playing second fiddle, Eddie slapped Wendy's hand in congratulations, seeming as genuinely pleased by the winnings shot as if it had been his own. Wendy, for her part, glowed luminously under the praise.

Was it possible, Nick wondered, that he could have been wrong about some of these kids? Now that he was finally beginning to see behind the garish trappings of their generation, they weren't turning out to be at all the way he'd expected— "Look out!"

Nick glanced up just in time to see the black-and-white patterned ball hurtling over the net in his direction. Too late to get his hands up into position, he reacted instinctively by "heading" the ball with a sharp twist of his neck. It bounced back over the net, then immediately died, dropping unreturnably to score the point.

"Hey, no fair!" Pete, the other team captain, cried hotly. "He hit that ball with his head, not his hands. This isn't a soccer game, you know!"

A heated debate ensued, which was settled only when Randy stepped in to mediate, and both teams finally agreed to replay the point. After that, Nick kept his mind on business and the game was quickly concluded in his team's favor. He accepted the laughing congratulations offered by the losing players, then bowed out quickly, joining Randy on the blanket before he could get roped into another game.

"Good work," said Randy, patting him on the shoulder with a smile. "I guess you showed those kids how it's done."

"Either that, or they showed me." Nick grinned ruefully as he lowered himself gingerly onto the sand. "Good Lord, I thought it would never end!"

"You mean to say you *weren't* having a great time up there?" Randy asked, shaking her head in mock dismay. "Why I would have thought that sort of thing was right up your alley—you know, setting a good parental example and all?"

Nick glared up at her balefully. "Are you making fun of me?"

"Who me?" Randy's smile was innocence itself. "Of course not."

"That's what I thought," Nick growled, trying to sound stern but not quite succeeding. Finally he simply gave up the effort, and they shared a companionable grin.

The sun had already begun its descent, and the day was cooling rapidly when Nick declared that it was time to head home.

"Oh daddy, do I have to?" Wendy asked plaintively. Her eyes strayed back to her group of friends who had moved farther down the beach where they were pulling stones in a circle, preparing to build a fire. "Everybody else is going to stay on, and Eddie said he'd be happy to give me a ride home later."

"Well..." Nick hedged, knowing it was time he made a decision. This was just the sort of situation he'd have avoided like the plague in the past. Yet ever since the night before, the things Randy had said had been weighing very heavily upon his mind. Indeed, once the volleyball game had ended, he'd found himself thinking of little else all afternoon.

The problem was, he had to admit that what she'd said made sense. Since the day of Wendy's birth fifteen years earlier, he *had* given her everything it was within his power to give. But how much would all that ultimately mean if he was unable to give her the one thing she needed the most— the freedom to grow and become the person she was meant to be?

It wouldn't be easy, Nick mused. With a sudden rush of insight, he realized that though he'd always told himself he was doing what was best for Wendy, in reality what he'd really been doing was what was best for himself. Protecting her as he had, he had taken the coward's way out, shielding her from the realities of growing up that he himself had not wanted to face.

That was, until last night, Nick reflected, when Randy had made him acknowledge his past once and for all. He'd known all along that Wendy and June were two entirely different people. Maybe it was time he stopped visiting one with the sins of the other. He'd raised his daughter to be a good, responsible girl. Deep down inside, where it mattered most, he did trust her. All at once he knew it was time to let her know that.

"I guess it will be all right," he said slowly, and felt a deep, unexpected sense of satisfaction at the way his daughter's eyes lit up with excitement.

"Thanks dad," Wendy cried, leaning down to brush a quick kiss across her father's cheek. "You're the greatest!" Spinning away, she dashed back across the sand to her friends.

"Wendy's right, you know," Randy said softly. She reached over and squeezed Nick's arm reassuringly, knowing what the simple act of faith had cost him. "You *are* the greatest."

"Oh lady," Nick drawled, turning to her with a teasing leer. "You ain't seen nothin' yet!"

They agreed they would drive back to Nick's house where, he promised her, Randy would be treated to the best grilled hamburgers this side of the Mississippi.

"How could I pass up an offer like that?" Randy asked laughingly, hopping out of the jeep as Nick pulled up beside the garage. "If you ask me, a barbeque sounds like the perfect end to a perfect day."

And it had been a perfect day, Randy mused several minutes later as she stood under the cool, stinging spray of the shower in Nick's guest bathroom. As perfect a day as any she could remember.

Tilting her head back into the spray as the water flowed down over her body, Randy reminisced about the fantasies of her childhood in which she and her family—a real family of which she was very much a part—would go on outings such as today's expedition to the lake. As a child she had never had the chance to know anything like the camaraderie that flowed so easily among this afternoon's group at the beach. Today she had reveled in the experience. For the first time, she had not been an outsider looking in, but rather an integral part of the proceedings. Never had anything felt so good.

And it was all Nick's doing, Randy mused. He was the one who had extended his small family to include her in its bosom; the one who had made her feel as though she truly belonged. When she was with him, she felt a sense of peace, of tranquility, unlike any she had known before.

She was in love with him, Randy realized suddenly. And the knowledge flowed over her with the warmth of molten honey, bringing a tingling sensation that she felt all the way down to her toes. For all the stern gruffness of the face he turned to the world, underneath she found a warm and caring man; one who was every bit as vulnerable as she herself.

Little by little he had revealed that inner facet of himself to her, and she had fallen further and further under his spell. Now the resolution was irrevocable. She belonged to Nick Jarros, Randy mused dreamily. She belonged *with* Nick Jarros, and she always would.

"Hey, hurry up in there, would you?" Nick called out, rapping on the bathroom door. "Dinner's almost ready!"

"Be right with you," Randy sang back, hurriedly rinsing the soap from her body and turning off the water.

Toweling off quickly, she slipped on a fresh T-shirt and pair of shorts that she had stowed in her beach bag. For once, she didn't bother with a bra, and the sensation of her firm, unfettered breasts bobbing beneath the light shirt left her feeling delightfully cool and free. Humming under her breath, she skipped down the stairs to join Nick in the kitchen.

"Well it's about time," said Nick. He was standing on the patio which led off from the kitchen, scooping two thick hamburgers up off the grill and onto their waiting buns. "I was beginning to think you'd gone and slipped out the front door while I wasn't looking."

"Not a chance," Randy scoffed, "I was just getting good and clean, that's all."

Nick turned to face her and his eyes traveled down the length of her body. Placing the two plates on the glass-topped table, he cleared his throat raggedly.

"I'm glad to see that, er...nothing shrank from being underwater all that time."

"So am I," Randy agreed, grinning wickedly. It was hard to miss the way his eyes were trained on her breasts as though he could not pull them away. "You know," she mused, slipping down into a seat at the table, "I'd have sworn you said you were a leg man."

"Yes...well..." Nick shook his head sharply, as though trying to clear it. Glancing up, he returned her grin. "Let's just say I'm a man who appreciates true greatness, no matter what form I find it in."

Over dinner they spoke of everything save the topic that was uppermost in both their minds—the tension that had been building steadily since they'd first seen each other that morning and which now made the air around them seem to hum and crackle with a life of its own.

"So tell me," said Nick, blurting out the first thing that rose to mind, "how's your job going these days?"

Pushing her food around her plate, Randy shrugged noncommittally. Down at the newspaper things had gone from bad to worse. For the most part, once the novelty of knowing who she was had worn off, the kids had stopped harassing her at home. But now with her anonymity shattered, Aunt Miranda's mail had begun to drop off precipitously. Already displeased by the furor her column had caused, the managing editor had taken to glowering sternly every time he passed her desk. That, however, was the last thing Randy felt like worrying about at the moment.

"Not bad," she replied, forcing down a bite or two of hamburger. "How about yours?"

To her everlasting relief, Nick launched into a long, drawn out explanation of the software package he was currently designing for a client on the West Coast, and Randy was able to sit back and simply listen, offering nothing to the conversation other than an occasional grunt, which seemed more than enough to satisfy him.

He was every bit as nervous as she was, she realized suddenly as Nick reached for a sip of wine and knocked the glass with his hand, nearly sending it flying off the table. While she was barely able to form a coherent sentence, it was clear that his edginess was manifesting itself in an inability to shut up. Randy smiled gently, finding his loquaciousness hopelessly endearing.

Dinner or no, she thought, surveying their still full plates, it was time for someone to take charge. Ever since that moment earlier at the lake, they had both known what was coming. Now she knew with certainty it was time.

"Nick?" she said, breaking into his monologue. "I think I'm finished eating, how about you?"

Startled from the discourse on new and innovative software designs in which he'd purposely buried himself, Nick glanced up in surprise. "What?

"I said," Randy repeated, rising from the table, "I think dinner's over. Why don't we go inside and listen to some music?"

"Oh yes...of course, if you'd like to," Nick stammered, rising as well. "That sounds fine. Let me just clear away these plates—"

"Leave them," Randy said quietly, taking his hand in hers. "We'll worry about them later."

As if in a dream, Nick followed her slowly back into the living room. Outside, the summer sun had finally set and the long shadows of night bathed the room in darkness.

It had been so long, he thought, watching the fluid swinging motion of her stride as she walked before him. And it was going to be so good....

Suddenly his nervousness vanished as he was filled with the rightness of what was about to happen between them. Never had he wanted anything so much as he desired the woman who was now standing before him, waiting patiently for his next move. That she wanted him, too, was written plainly in her clear brown eyes. The realization made his temperature soar.

When he reached out to draw her to him, she floated into his arms with a soft sigh that spoke of many things—of longing, of needing and of coming home.

"Oh Randy," he murmured, nuzzling her soft, silky hair. "I can't believe this is finally happening."

"Nor can I," Randy replied. She nestled closer against his chest, wrapping her arms tightly about his waist and holding him to her.

Her eyelids fluttered shut as his mouth lowered slowly to hers, tasting the sweetness of her full pink lips. His tongue traced their outline and then, as they parted beneath his caress, plunged deep inside with a thrust that Randy felt as a lightening jolt of sensation that shimmered throughout her entire body.

His hand came up to cradle the back of her head, holding her steady as his tongue withdrew and thrust again and then again. Bracing back against him, Randy moaned aloud. Her body was throbbing, filled with a languid heaviness that left her weak and breathless. She clung to him, grasping the hard muscle of his buttocks in her palms and grinding him toward the ache in the center of her body.

Nick needed no encouragement to deepen the embrace, and now his thigh slid between hers. He shifted slightly and Randy felt the hard sinew of his leg pressed against her. Instinctively she responded by rubbing up against him, uttering a soft, whimpering cry as she writhed within his hands.

My God, thought Nick, feeling as though he held a flaming firebrand in his hands. Never had he known a woman whose passions ignited so quickly, and this knowledge of her arousal spurred his own as nothing else could have.

"This time," he whispered, "everything is going to be perfect."

Drawing her head back to gaze up into his eyes, Randy smiled slowly. "I'm here," she said. "You're here. It already is."

Then her eyes widened as a sudden thought struck her. "Nick, did you lock the front door?" She saw him frown, and knew what his answer would be.

"I did, but Wendy has a key." His hands slid down the length of her body as he swept her suddenly up into his arms. "She also," he added, his eyes glinting wickedly, "has the good sense not to intrude when I've closed the doors in my part of the house. What do you say we move this party to my bedroom where we can be sure we won't be interrupted?"

"Good idea," Randy smiled as he strode quickly down the hall.

Once there, Nick lowered her to her feet beside the wide bed. Without relinquishing their contact, he slid his hands back up to her waist where he grasped the hem of her T-shirt and pulled it slowly over her head. Randy smiled shyly as his breath escaped in a long, drawn out sigh.

"They're not..." she said, hesitating painfully, "too big?"

"They're not," Nick repeated, his hands coming up to stroke her tenderly, almost reverently, "too big." The look of smoldering desire she read in his eyes told her everything she needed to know. "They are beautiful. You are beautiful. You're all the woman a man could ever need."

Stepping back for only a moment, Nick divested himself quickly of his clothes. Then he came to her once more, his fingers slipping inside the waistband of her shorts to peel them down over her hips and away. As one, they sank down together onto the bed.

For a moment, Nick was content to simply stare, to drink in the sight of her beautiful, long-limbed body, gleaming in the soft blush of the moonlight that flowed through the windows beside the bed. Then, as though a dam had burst inside him, he wanted to be everywhere at once—touching, caressing, tasting, learning all the secret delights that her body had to offer.

His head dipped down to nestle between her soft breasts, his tongue finding the already swollen nipples and bathing them gently. His hands slid lower, then lower still across the flat plane of her midriff to the nest of curls beneath. Randy gasped sharply as his fingers found the core of her feminity, stroking her until the fires that burned throughout her body threatened to consume her with their heat.

"Love me, Nick," she cried, her head whipping back and forth on the pillow. "Love me please."

"I will," Nick promised fervently, and in that instant he realized the blinding truth of his words. Then Randy twisted urgently beneath him, reaching, then pulling him up to cover her and the moment was gone. Nothing existed save the exquisite rush of sensation that pulsated throughout his body as he slowly made them one.

He tried to take it slowly. He wanted so badly for it to last. But Randy met his measured thrusts with an eagerness that chased him faster...and then faster still. Randy cried out sharply, arching beneath him. He felt the flutter of the small spasms that rippled through her pulling him closer, ever closer to the edge.

Then ecstasy burst upon him with the blazing intensity of a wildfire burning out of control, and Nick lost himself in the release.

Lying quietly beside him, it was a long time before Randy was able to even breathe, let alone think.

So much the better, she decided, making no attempt to sort out the jumble of thoughts that was running through her mind. For the moment, she had no desire to worry what the future might bring. It was enough to simply lie, cradled in Nick's arms, and savor what had happened between them.

"I'm sorry," Nick said softly. His hand reached out to tangle through the soft silky strands of her hair, stroking her head as he held her to him.

"Sorry?" Randy gasped in surprise. "What on earth for?"

Nick shook his head slowly. There were so many things he wanted to say—how unexpectedly she'd taken over a part of his life, how much she had come to mean to him—and none of them seemed right. The situation was entirely of his own making, and yet it was impossible. He wasn't ready to marry again. For Wendy's sake, he could not condone something less.

Nor, Nick realized, could he forget the way they had met. Though he'd tried to put it out of his mind, the spectre of her job still lurked between them with its disturbing reminders of his first marriage. He simply could not go through something like that again.

Knowing all that, he should never have taken her to bed, Nick mused. He should never have allowed things to get so far out of control...

"Nick?" Randy raised herself up on one elbow to look down into his eyes questioningly.

"I'm sorry," he said again, stung by the inadequacy of his words. "I never meant to rush you."

Randy smiled softly. "Is that all?" she said, relaxing visibly. "I guess in that case, I'd better apologize to you as well."

Nick frowned. "What do you mean?"

Randy gazed down at him, her amusement obvious. "Oh Nick, couldn't you tell that I was in every bit as big a hurry as you were?"

"Well..."

Shaking her head, Randy reached up to stroke his jaw, tilting his face to hers. Slowly, she brushed her lips across his. "I know I've told you time and again that you're being too hard on Wendy," she murmured. "But has it ever occurred to you that you're being too hard on yourself as well? No matter how hard you try, you simply can't take responsibility for everything that happens."

"I don't—" Nick began, but Randy quieted him with a finger across his lips.

"You do. You've got to stop blaming yourself for something that happened a long time ago. Everybody makes mistakes, and you've done everything possible to rectify yours. When are you going to realize that nobody's perfect?''

"Is that what you think," Nick asked, "that I'm trying to live up to some impossible standard that I can't hope to achieve?''

Randy hesitated, drawing a deep breath and then slowly releasing it before answering. All at once, she knew that whatever she said to him now would shape the future of their whole relationship. "There are areas of your life," she said finally, "where I think you try too hard—"

"Like Wendy's upbringing," Nick interjected, and Randy slowly nodded.

"I admire the effort you make, but sometimes I just wish that you could relax a little, realize that no matter how hard you try, you can't control every eventuality. You do the best you can, let that be enough."

Frowning, Nick shook his head slowly. Sometimes, he thought, doing your best simply wasn't enough. He wanted more, he wanted everything to be just right—for Wendy and now, he was finding, for Randy as well. Yet he couldn't seem to make it happen....

"I love you, Nick," Randy whispered softly, almost inaudibly, and for a moment his heart seemed to stop within his breast as he wondered whether he had heard her right.

"You do?" he asked, then frowned at the inanity of the question.

"Yes." Randy nodded, and the simplicity of her declaration moved him greatly.

He knew the response she wanted to hear, knew he had only to open his mouth and say the words to bring her the same sort of joy she had brought to him. Then unexpectedly Wendy's face floated before him, and he found he could not speak at all.

Even as he hesitated, he knew the moment was gone. Whatever he might say now would have the hollow ring of being forced. It would sound like a concession to the moment and nothing more. He could not, would not, cheapen what they had shared that way.

It was better not to speak at all, Nick decided. Instead he let his actions speak for him, using the arm that circled Randy's shoulders to pull her to him as his other hand began to stroke her body rythmically, rekindling the passion that had flowed between them.

This time their lovemaking was slow and gentle, suffused with emotions that went far beyond the physical joy they found in each other's bodies. Shuddering in the aftermath of his release, Nick knew a satisfaction that transcended any he had ever known.

Clasping her to him fiercely, he wondered how he would ever be able to let her go.

Nine

Dear Aunt Miranda,

I know there are a lot of girls who wouldn't think that I have a problem at all, but I do. I know this is going to sound strange, but I am *too* popular. I have more dates than I can handle, as many as I want to accept for every night of the week.

I am only sixteen years old, but I have always been very grown up for my age, if you know what I mean. I enjoy going out, and I enjoy having a good time. Now, however, I am beginning to wonder if all this running around is ruining my reputation.

The very first time I go out with a guy, he seems to think it is okay to drive to some secluded spot where we can park and make out. Sometimes it seems as though that's the only thing my dates are interested in at all. I'll admit that in the past, I've usually gone along, but now

my girlfriends tell me they are beginning to hear stories about me that just aren't true. It's getting so that
now every time a new guy asks me out, I wonder how
much he's heard, and what he really has in mind.

You've got to tell me, Aunt Miranda. Can I still sal-
vage my reputation, or is it already too late?

Signed,
Worried By The Gossip

Dear Worried,

From the sounds of your letter, you have every right
to be concerned. A reputation is a very fragile commodity. Once lost or damaged, it can be almost impossible to regain. Just by recognizing the problem,
however, you have taken the first step in the right
direction.

The most important thing for you to do now, is to
give those gossips no further fuel to talk about. You're
going to have to decide how *you* want to live your life,
and then set about wiping the slate clean and making a
fresh start. You may not see results right away, but believe me, in time they will come.

Good luck. I'll be rooting for you!

Signed,
Aunt Miranda

"Hey Randy, Hank wants to see you in his office right
away."

Still caught up in the response she'd just finished composing, Randy glanced up as Bonnie stuck her head in the
door to the back office. She nodded absently as she rolled
the sheet of paper out of her typewriter, clipped it to the
letter and set them both aside.

Now what? she wondered irritably. Hank, the paper's managing editor had been on her case every day for the last two weeks, ever since Nick's fateful slip had given her away. What more could he possibly have to complain about now?

"Somehow," she muttered wryly under her breath, "I have a sneaking suspicion this just isn't gong to be my day."

But then yesterday hadn't exactly been her day either, nor the day before. It had been forty-eight hours now since she'd seen Nick—two long nights since she'd lain in his arms and they'd made glorious love then slept nestled side by side until long past dawn.

She'd been late for work that morning, Randy remembered with a smile. Because even in the harsh light of the morning after, when she'd awoken to the knowledge that Nick didn't love her, that he couldn't love her the way that she loved him, she still had been unable to tear herself away.

It had taken the unmistakable sounds of Wendy rising and showering in her room on the floor above them to bring her back to her senses. Nick had looked visibly nervous at the prospect of his daughter and his lover coming face to face under such compromising circumstances. Hoping that he wouldn't accept, Randy had volunteered to slip out the back before Wendy made an appearance.

To her chagrin, Nick had pounced upon the offer as a godsend, handing her the keys to the Ferrari as he escorted her hurriedly to the door. Their parting kiss had been brief and awkward. To Randy it had seemed as though not a single trace of the warmth and caring Nick had shown her the night before remained.

And now, she thought dispiritedly, two whole days had passed without a word. She'd thought of calling him. Indeed, there had been times when she'd had to fight to restrain the impulse to pick up the receiver and dial his number. Only the memory of that night, when she had

confessed the depth of her feelings to him and he had offered nothing in return had kept her from completing the
call. If their relationship was to have any sort of future at
all, Randy realized, the next move was going to have to be
his.

"Randy, hurry up!" Bonnie hissed, and Randy looked up
in surprise to find the receptionist standing before her desk,
a frown clouding her normally animated features. "He's in
a bad enough mood already. Keeping him waiting is only
going to make things worse!"

"All right, all right," Randy grumbled, rising to her feet.
"I'm coming."

She found Hank sitting in the large leather swivel chair
behind his desk, waiting for her. As she entered the office
and closed the door behind her, he lifted a small stack of
letters, then let them fall from his fingers, one by one, to
scatter carelessly about the blotter.

"Do you see these?"

Randy nodded, refusing to be intimidated by his blunt
stare.

"These letters," Hank announced, gesturing toward the
meager collection disparagingly, "represent the sum total of
the mail your column has drawn in the last two days."

"Yes, I know," Randy replied, not knowing what more
there was to say.

"Good, then maybe you'll understand why I'm so upset.
Damn it, Randy, the mailroom tells me that we used to bring
these letters in by the truckload. So what's going on?"

"Do you mind if I sit down?"

Hank nodded, and Randy drew up a chair before his
desk. "As I know you're aware," she said, choosing her
words carefully, "there was a small problem several weeks
ago over the secret of Aunt Miranda's identity. You know
how kids are, once the secret was out, they felt obliged to

make the most of it. Now, however—'' Randy paused for a
small shrug ''—the novelty of knowing who I am seems to
have worn off. Rather than gloating over the access they
have to me, the kids are beginning to worry about just how
much access I have to them.''

''Oh for Pete's sake.'' Hank scowled. ''Give it to me in
plain English, would you?''

''Very simply,'' said Randy. ''The teenagers who pour out
their problems to Aunt Miranda are afraid that their secrets are no longer safe. Obviously it was one thing to write
in when their letters were going to be read by a stranger,
quite another when the person they're confiding in is a
known quantity. After all, I work with these kids, and I've
gotten to know some of them quite well. I imagine they're
afraid that after reading their letters I'm going to be trying
to second guess who they are.''

''I see,'' said Hank, nodding slowly. ''But unfortunately, understanding the problem doesn't change the solution. You know the policy. We're a small paper in a small
town. We can't afford to carry any dead weight. Any regular feature that loses its readership is out.''

''But—!'' Randy gasped. ''You can't be serious!''

Hank shrugged apologetically. ''I'm afraid so. Listen, this
is no more my fault than it is yours. Tell me what else I'm
going to do.'' His eyes narrowed as he stared at her
thoughtfully. ''Don't worry, you're not going to be out of
a job. That isn't what I had in mind at all. Your work here
has always been good. Not only that, but you're smart and
reliable, too, and that isn't easy to find these days. Just because the column goes doesn't mean that you're out as well.
I'm sure we can find something else for you to do. Maybe
advertising sales, or layout....''

Randy shut her eyes briefly, wishing that she could cover
her ears as well. She didn't want to hear what he was say-

ing, didn't want to believe that this could really be happening to her. Sure it was nice to know that she still had a job, but that wasn't what really mattered. What mattered was the way the kids had needed Aunt Miranda, and she had needed them.

That column was important. It meant everything to her. She refused to give it up without a fight.

"There must be something we can do," she said desperately, casting about in her mind for an answer. "After all, it isn't as though the readership has dried up entirely."

Hank's gaze flickered tellingly downward over the meager collection of letters.

"All right," Randy said quickly, "so things have gotten a little sparse at the moment. That doesn't mean they won't turn back around. You know how kids are. Today's hot topic is tomorrow's old news. Why, I'll bet in a couple of weeks, they won't even remember what all the furor was all about."

For a long moment, Hank said nothing at all, but simply sat, studying her pensively from across the desk. "All right," he said finally. "I don't want you to think I'm being entirely unreasonable about this. And who knows, maybe things will happen just like you say. But just in case they don't, I'm going to take out a little insurance.

"As of this Friday, this column is out for the next two weeks. We'll use that time to see what kind of response you get, both pro and con. If at the end, things have picked up again, you're back in business. If not..." Hank shrugged meaningfully.

"Thank you," Randy said sincerely, grateful for any concession she could get. She wasn't out of the woods yet by a long shot, but she was a damn sight closer than she had been a few minutes ago. A two-week reprieve wasn't much, but it was better than nothing!

"You'll see," she said, arming her voice with a confidence that was far from what she felt inside. "The kids love Aunt Miranda. They'll want her back."

"I hope so," said Hank, not sounding entirely convinced. To Randy's surprise, he draped a fatherly arm around her shoulder as he ushered her from the office. "For your sake, I hope you're right."

That evening, Randy ate a solitary dinner in front of the television. She watched with only half-hearted interest as the villainess of her favorite night-time soap plotted and schemed her way through another episode, only to be foiled by the goodness of her ex-husband's second wife in the end.

If only life were really that easy, she thought with a sigh as she switched off the set. If only her problems could be so neatly tied up and disposed of. But no, rather than diminishing, they seemed to be growing with each passing day. As if the problems she was having at work weren't bad enough, then there was the far more important matter of Nick.

Why hadn't he called, she wondered unhappily. She leaned back into the soft couch, hugging one of the plump throw pillows to her chest. She'd gone over and over that night they'd spent together in her mind. Unpalatable as it was, she could reach only one conclusion. She must have driven him away with that artless and unexpected declaration of her love.

That had to be it, Randy mused, deciding that he had misread the situation entirely. Rather than hearing the spontaneous and joyous admission it was meant to be, Nick must have felt that she was trying to pressure him in some way. That much, Randy realized now, should have been obvious by his lack of response.

But at that time, she had been so caught up in the heady thrust of her own emotions, she'd scarcely even noticed. It wasn't until the next morning, and then the two long days that had followed, that she'd realized the extent of his withdrawal. Now, Randy thought, feeling a sudden burst of pain that knifed sharply through her midsection, she couldn't help but wonder if she'd ever hear from him again.

Listlessly, Randy picked up the evening paper lying on the coffee table. She turned to her column and read slowly through it. Unless something drastic happened, Aunt Miranda would make her farewell appearance at the end of the week. The letters she'd replied to that afternoon were scheduled to run in the last column on Friday.

It just didn't seem fair, thought Randy. She was so good at sorting out everyone else's lives, why did she do such a hopelessly bad job when it came to her own?

A weak smile crossed her face as she sat back and fancifully composed a letter detailing her own woes.

Dear Aunt Miranda,
  My whole world is falling apart and I don't know what to do. I am on the verge of losing a job that means everything to me. I'm afraid I may have already lost a man who means even more. I was happy for a while. All I ever truly wanted was to belong, and I thought I'd finally found that here...

"Phooey!" Randy spat out emphatically. If someone sent her a letter that reeked so atrociously of self-pity, she knew exactly what sort of a response she'd fire back!

Dear Martyr,
  Take it from me, nothing ever got accomplished by sitting around feeling sorry for yourself. The first thing you've got to do is get up off your butt and get moving! So you think you've lost everything, do you? Then maybe it's time to make a fresh start.

Why not take a couple of days off and get away? With time and distance, you may view the situation in a whole new perspective. It certainly can't hurt...

No it couldn't, could it? Randy mused, liking the idea more and more. In fact it sounded like just the thing she needed. Maybe it was high time she took her own advice after all!

The decision made, it only took her until the following afternoon to tie up the remaining loose ends. Since the column was already written through its projected ending date, Hank was more than happy to give her the vacation she requested. When work ended, she went straight to the high school, where she explained to the soccer team that she was taking a week off for personal reasons, and that a substitute coach would be running them through their paces in the meantime.

"You will be coming back, won't you?" Wendy asked, stopping by Randy's car when practice ended.

"Of course," Randy replied, smiling down at the girl reassuringly. No matter what happened between her and Nick, she hoped that it wouldn't affect the friendship she'd forged with Wendy over the past several weeks. The girl needed the guiding presence of a woman in her life, and it was a role that Randy had stepped into gladly. For Wendy's sake, as well as her own, she did not want to see it end. "I'll be back before you even have time to miss me, promise."

"I'll hold you to that," Wendy said firmly, and Randy was surprised by the look of adult determination that crossed the teenager's face. "Dad and I need you, you know."

"Yes, well..." Randy stammered, dismayed by the hot tears she felt gathering in the corners of her eyes. Impulsively she leaned down and gathered Wendy into a quick hug. ''I need you, too, sweetheart,'' she whispered. ''Believe me, I just have to have some time alone, to get a few things sorted out in my mind. But I'll be back, you can count on that.''

She was in her car driving toward home when the tears began to fall.

''Sir, would you like another drink?''

Nick looked up from the sheaf of papers he'd spread out on the small plastic tray into the smiling face of the friendly flight attendant. ''No thanks, I'm all set.''

''Sorry about the delay,'' she said, continuing on down the narrow aisle with her cart. ''But the captain assures me that we'll be landing soon.''

''Good.'' Nick nodded absently. The plane, a shuttle on which he had flown down to Washington on Monday evening, had been in a holding pattern over Hartford's Bradley Airport for the last hour.

Just like the rest of his life, Nick mused grimly. He glanced down at the report spread out before him and realized he hadn't the slightest idea what it said. Swearing irritably under his breath, he gathered up the papers and dumped them unceremoniously in his briefcase.

What was happening to him anyway, he wondered. For the last three days, it seemed as though his life had been in constant turmoil. He wasn't eating, he wasn't sleeping, and now he couldn't even focus on his work. It was all Randy Wade's fault.

Scarcely even aware that he was smiling, Nick remembered how she had looked that morning awakening in his arms—her red-gold hair fanned out across his pillow, her features dreamy and relaxed with sleep, her body curled languidly to mold itself to his. If it hadn't been for Wendy, stirring on the floor above them, he'd have been content to remain in bed all day.

But his daughter did exist. She was a cherished and irrefutable part of his life. It was her presence that had made him so reluctant to venture another commitment, Nick told himself as Randy pulled on her clothes and slipped away. For Wendy's sake, he simply could not afford to make another mistake.

But over dinner that evening, his daughter had surprised him.

"We need to talk," he'd begun hesitantly, wondering how he was going to broach the topic that had been on his mind all day.

"I'll say we do," Wendy replied, grinning mischievously. "Don't you know it's impolite to send a lady home the morning after without even offering her breakfast?"

"What?" Nick's mouth gaped open comically. "How do you know about that?"

"Da-addy!" Wendy rolled her eyes heavenward in exasperation. "I am not a child, you know. Give me some credit. Besides," she added, still grinning, "I saw Randy driving away in your car after you hustled her out the door."

For a moment, Nick could think of nothing at all to say. Instead he simply sat, staring at his daughter across the table in bemused surprise.

"So," Wendy prompted, "are you going to make an honest woman out of her or not?"

He'd be damned if he knew what he was going to say to that, Nick remembered. But thankfully, he had been saved by the bell—the ringing of the telephone to be exact. Wendy had answered the call in the other room. He was unable to hear what she was saying, but only a few minutes had passed until she was calling him to pick up the extension and speak to his ex-wife.

When he'd gotten on, June had sounded desperate, embroiled supposedly in a crisis from which only he could extricate her. Nick had fallen for her pitch, hook, line, and sinker. He'd hopped a plane to Washington that evening, only to spend the next thirty-six hours realizing what a mistake he had made.

Oh, she'd been desperate all right, Nick mused bitterly. Desperate not to lose him to the arms of another woman. For reasons he couldn't begin to fathom, after all these years of estrangement, she had taken the news of his relationship with Randy as a challenge to her femininity. It had taken him a day and a half to see through her scheme and to realize that the "help" she had in mind wasn't the sort he had any intention of giving.

Then again, Nick reflected, June may have set him up, but it wasn't exactly as though she had forced him to come. No, looking back now, he could see that when her frantic request had been made, he'd grabbed the excuse it offered eagerly. It wasn't that he'd been running to help where he was needed, Nick realized suddenly, but he'd been running away from Randy and all that their growing relationship entailed.

Nick frowned abruptly, realizing for the second time in the past few days what a coward he had been. At least this interlude in Washington had served one purpose—it had brought him to his senses with a jolt. Seeing June again, he had realized suddenly that the mistake he was making lay not in what he was doing, but in what he hadn't done.

Ever since he and Randy had first met, he'd been holding back, supplying one excuse after another, and building up all the reasons in his mind why he was sure that their relationship could never work. He'd been hurt once, he told himself. Determined never to put himself in that position again, he'd even gone so far as to deny feelings that he now knew were very real.

How many times had he used his daughter as a convenient buffer between them, Nick mused. Even worse, how many times had he told himself that Randy and June were too much alike, and that getting involved with a woman like that was one mistake he never intended to make again?

Nick's lips twisted in a bitter smile. If these last two days had shown him anything, it was how wrong he had been on that score. Randy and his ex-wife had almost nothing in common at all. June's involvement was purely selfish. She threw herself into causes to the detriment of people. Randy's causes *were* people. Her warmth and her caring were evident in everything she did. So why hadn't he seen the difference sooner?

Because he hadn't wanted to see, Nick mused grimly. It wasn't until that night in her house when they'd been interrupted by yet another teenager seeking advice that he'd begun to understand, if only subconsciously, what was going on. Even then, he'd responded by fighting it, by storming out of her life again. But the truth he'd been forced to see was clear—Randy wasn't butting, unasked, into other people's lives. No, they were coming to her. Those kids, including his own daughter, really needed Aunt Miranda.

Just as he himself needed Randy Wade.

Nick sighed softly. He could see now that what he'd done was take the coward's way out, not only with Wendy, but with his own life as well. After June had left them, he had tried so hard to protect them both—never letting anyone close enough so that he or Wendy would run the risk of being hurt again.

Then Randy had come along and everything had changed. Just as she had made him see how important it was for Wendy to be allowed to experience things for herself, so too had she made him realize how thoroughly he'd succeeded in cutting himself off from all that life had to offer.

He'd finally freed his daughter from that snug, secure nest he'd made for them both, Nick mused. Wasn't it about time for him to leave it himself?

Above him, the Fasten Seatbelts sign flashed on, indicating that the plane was finally going to land. Three whole days of silence, thought Nick. Randy must really be wondering what had happened to him. But tonight, as soon as he got home, he would give her a call. Though it was late, with any luck she might even invite him over. Nick smiled at the prospect. He couldn't wait to see her again. Then they could get everything straightened out once and for all.

When he got home, Wendy greeted him at the door.

"You've really blown it this time, Dad. What's the matter, did you forget to take a dime for the phone, or what?"

"What are you talking about?" Nick asked, his expression mirroring his confusion as he set his overnight bag down in the hall. "I called you last night to make sure everything was all right. Besides, you always knew where you could reach me."

"Not me," Wendy said with a frown. "Randy. Why didn't you call and let *her* know where you were?"

Nick grinned. Just the mention of her name sent a quick shaft of elation darting through him.

"To tell the truth, once I'd given my darling daughter a hug..." he said, gathering Wendy into his arms for a quick squeeze, "that was going to be the very next thing on my list."

"Well, you'd better be quick about it," Wendy announced ominously. "Did you know she was planning to leave town?"

"Leave?" Nick said sharply. He turned to his daughter with a frown. "Where is she going?"

Wendy shrugged lightly, acting her part to the hilt. Her father meant well, but sometimes he could be so...cautious, especially when it came to things like this. Look how much time he'd already wasted.

"She didn't say, but I bet it's some place far, far away...." Wendy let her voice trail away meaningfully, noting with satisfaction her father's response.

"Oh no, she doesn't," Nick roared, striding back to the door. "She won't get away from me that easily."

"Bye Dad," Wendy called gaily, watching from the porch as her father strode down the steps to his car. As the Ferrari roared away down the drive, she added with a mischievous smile, "Don't worry, I won't bother waiting up."

Randy had just about finished packing in preparation for the early start she planned to get the next morning when she heard the pounding on her front door.

"Randy!" came the unmistakable, throaty sound of Nick's voice. "Randy, are you in there? Open this door!"

"Coming!" Randy called, trying to ignore the treacherous way her heart leapt at the sound of his voice. She hurried to the door and flung it open, wondering what all the commotion was about.

"Thank God," Nick muttered, stepping inside and gathering her into his arms. "I'm not too late. You haven't left yet."

Too late, Randy thought wonderingly. What on earth was he talking about?

Then the thought fled as, with a small sigh, she relaxed and simply gave herself up to the sensual pleasure of being held in Nick's embrace. His body was warm and hard, its faint musky aroma reaching out to tantalize her senses.

Contentedly, Randy buried her face in his shirtfront and inhaled deeply.

This was what she had spent the last three days wanting, aching for, needing. It was as though by his very presence, Nick had banished the emptiness that surrounded her, and made her whole again. For a moment, Randy didn't even stop to consider why he was there. It was enough that he had come.

She looked up, blinking slowly, as Nick grasped her shoulders and disentangled them gently. He stepped back and closed the front door, then taking her hand, led the way to the living room where they sat down, side by side, on the couch.

"Thank God, you're still here," Nick repeated feelingly. He squeezed her hand warmly in his. "I was so afraid you'd already be gone."

Randy shrugged. "I considered going tonight, but then I decided it was probably better to get an early start in the morning."

"Oh no you don't," Nick said forcibly. His grip on her hand tightened, as if by merely holding on, he would be able to prevent the impending separation. "You're not moving away from Glendale, and that's that."

Randy looked up in surprise. What was he talking about now? "No," she said slowly, "you're right, I'm not."

Now it was Nick's turn to look baffled. "You're not?"

"No, of course not. Whatever gave you that idea?"

"Why that little minx," Nick muttered, shaking his head in rueful comprehension.

"What?" Randy peered up into his eyes curiously.

"Nothing." Nick said with a quick grin. Now that he knew she wasn't running away from him, he felt the desperation that had haunted him for the past half hour begin to slowly seep away. Still smiling, he relaxed back against the cushions of the couch, cradling Randy to his side. Then all at once a sudden thought struck him.

"If you're not leaving Glendale," he asked, "then where *are* you going?"

Randy frowned slightly, trying unsuccessfully to gauge his mood. "I just thought maybe I needed some time alone, that's all. A friend offered me her cottage on Cape Cod for the next two weeks, and I accepted."

"But what about your job? Surely you can't just pick up and leave like that on a moment's notice?"

"My job," said Randy, sighing softly, "seems to be in limbo at the moment. The paper had decided to pull the column for the next two weeks anyway, so I'm afraid I won't be missed at all."

"That's where you're wrong," Nick murmured. His hand came up to cup the sides of her jaw, tilting her face to his. "I, for one, will miss you terribly."

Randy gulped down the lump that had risen in her throat. "You will?"

"Umm-hmm." Nick nodded. His mouth descended to brush lightly over hers. "Now that I'm back from Washington—"

"Washington?" Randy repeated, her eyes widening. Was *that* why she hadn't heard anything from him? "What were you doing there?"

Frowning, Nick raked the fingers of one hand back through his hair. "That's not important now. What is important, is getting everything straightened out between us. I meant to talk to Wendy about us when I got home, but there just wasn't time. You see I wanted her to be the first to know about our engagement—"

"Engagement?" Randy shrieked, sitting up suddenly. "What engagement?"

"Oh yes." Nick nodded. "I guess I forgot to ask, didn't I?"

"Yes, you did," Randy replied firmly, but the gleam that twinkled suddenly in her tawny eyes belied the severity of the words.

"You see, I asked Wendy—"

"You did?" Randy's eyebrows lifted. He'd put her through enough torture over the last three days that she wasn't above getting some of her own back. "And did she say yes?"

"Well of course." Damn, thought Nick. This conversation was getting entirely out of hand!

"Well then," Randy teased lightly. "I hope you and she will be very happy together."

Nick scowled. "That's not what I meant, and you know it!"

"It isn't?" Randy smiled innocently.

"No, of course not!"

"Then," Randy said softly, the laughter vanishing suddenly from her face, "just what did you mean, Nick?"

Slowly Nick reached up to thread his fingers through the long silky strands of her hair, lifting them up in a gentle motion as he slipped them behind her ear. Randy's scalp tingled beneath his touch as he continued to stroke her absently. She watched his features relax and soften, until he was smiling down at her gently.

"I meant to say that I love you," Nick murmured. "And to ask you to be my wife."

"Yes!" Randy cried, her voice growing in volume as she threw herself into his arms for an exuberant hug. "Yes, yes, yes and yes!"

Now it was Nick's eyes that twinkled mischievously. "Does that mean you accept?"

"Would you like to hear my answer again?" Randy asked, preparing herself for another rendition.

Teasingly, Nick held his hands over his ears. "I don't think so," he demurred. "This may be one of those cases where once is enough."

"For you, maybe," Randy said, "but not for me. Tell me you love me Nick. I want to hear you say those words again."

"I love you," Nick murmured softly. "I will always love you, and I will always need you in my life. You know that, don't you?"

Slowly Randy nodded, loving the sincerity she read in his eyes, the solid ring of truth she heard in his words. "I love you, too," she answered softly.

Her eyelids fluttered shut as Nick lowered his head to hers and she parted her lips for his kiss. Her heart seemed to expand, filled with a joy and sense of wonder she had longed for but never found. At long last, Randy had come home.

Dear Aunt Miranda,

Boy am I glad to see that the powers that be finally wised up and put your column back in the paper. We kids have really missed it over the last two weeks. (What else did we have to whisper about during English Lit, ha, ha!) I guess those letters we sent in to complain may have done some good after all.

Anyway, I just wanted to let you know that we're on your side. I don't have any problems for you to handle at the moment, but it's nice to know that you'll be there for me when I do. Keep up the good work!

Signed,
A Member of
Boring Mr. Blake's
English Lit Class

P.S. You may not remember me, but I was the guy who wrote in because he was too shy to go out with girls. You gave me lots of advice about the zoo and all, and so far, it has worked great. Now that things are going so well, I only have one more question: How do I get to the petting zoo from here?

Silhouette Desire

Silhouette Desire

COMING NEXT MONTH

A MUCH NEEDED HOLIDAY
Joan Hohl

When Kate saw a child lost among the shoppers, she vowed to give the parent a piece of her mind. But what began as a contest of wills between Trace and Kate, became a victory of love, giving their hungry hearts a much needed holiday.

MOONLIGHT SERENADE
Laurel Evans

Emma ran a radio station in Connecticut and when Simon invited her to give a speech, she refused. But when he kept returning at weekends, Emma fell in love. Surely such a hotshot would never be content with her...?

HERO AT LARGE
Aimee Martel

Leslie had to convince Ted Logan that her mission to save the reputation of his school was as important as his job to rescue downed pilots. But capturing his heart would be her biggest mission.

COMING NEXT MONTH

TEACHER'S PET
Ariel Berk

Cecily was settling into life as a teacher when Nick began to unsettle things. For both, it was a time for their hearts to speak — and their minds to listen.

HOOK, LINE AND SINKER
Elaine Camp

Roxie was a reporter for Sportspeople, but an expert fisherwoman? Never! She has to deceive Sonny to get an interview with him. But when she fell in love with him, she knew she had to tell him the truth. She just couldn't let him be the one that got away.

LOVE BY PROXY
Diana Palmer

Fired for belly dancing in front of her boss. Amanda was then offered a job as a companion to his mother. Worth hadn't ignored her beauty, but he was determined to bid for her on his own terms.

APRIL TITLES

Can anyone tame Tamara?

Life is one long party for the outrageous Tamara.

Not for her wedded bliss and domesticity.

Fiercely independent and determined to stay that way, her one goal is to make a success of her acting career.

Then, during a brief holiday with her sister, Tamara's life is turned upside down by Jake DeBlais, man of the world and seducer of women…

Discover love in full bloom in this exciting sequel to Arctic Rose, by Claire Harrison.

Available from May 1986.
Price £2.25.

W⦿RLDWIDE